Advanced praise for This and That but Mostly the Other

In *This and That but Mostly the Other,* Shane accomplishes to acquaint us with his diverse writing talent. Each piece penetrates deep into the mind with a power to move us from one realm to another leaving those who read this book with multiple candidates as their favourite.

Ann Edall-Robson
Author - The Quiet Spirits

Insightful and relatable - each piece showcases everyday life through a unique combination of curiosity and concerns. The collection is a personal commentary on loss, love, and opportunity as seen through the eyes of a true observer.

Kaleigh Kanary

We live in an age where we can easily say, "it's been done." But what Kroetsch accomplishes is nothing less than a totally unique dream sequence. Each story, be it two paragraphs long or eight pages, is a vivid and engaging dream sequence. The images conjured all feel like a waking dream, and it's incredible. The short stories make you ache for more, and that is truly a beautiful rarity. I would love to be in the author's head for forty-five minutes. I'd get absolutely nothing done, but damn it would be interesting.

Ian G.

Shane Kroetsch is an inspired and insightful writer. The book *This and That But Mostly the Other* takes Shane's readers on a thought provoking journey of short stories. I have often wondered about the people around me, what their thoughts are, and what their day to day lives are like. I found answers in these stories, and then some! The characters are well developed, and the writing evokes emotional and even physical reactions in the reader. I found tears falling in some pages, and goosebumps raised in others. Shane is a writer who produces riveting tales of experiences that any everyday person could possibly encounter, some a blessing, others a chilling nightmare. I cannot wait to read it again!

Jenn Rasmussen

This and That but Mostly the Other

Shane Kroetsch

This and That But Mostly the Other
Copyright © Shane Kroetsch

First edition 2019

Pencil on Paper
Airdrie, Alberta
Canada
www.pencilonpaper.ca

ISBN 978-1-9994820-0-8 (paperback)
ISBN 978-1-9994820-1-5 (ebook)

Cover design by Sarah Ng, Sarah Burk, and Shane Kroetsch
Author photo by Sarah Ng(https://www.flickr.com/people/ngsarah/)

Printed and bound in the United States of America by IngramSpark

For Alicia and the boys.
I hope you always have the courage to follow your dreams.

Contents

THIS

No Ordinary Thursday

I remember feeling nauseous. The bus would vault forward and then a few hundred feet later grind to a halt. The driver must have been having a bad day. I don't remember much else about the ride. It could have been that I was focused on not missing my stop, or maybe it was something else.

Work was taking a lot out of me. There comes a point where 'do more with less' stretches people too thin. I was having trouble sleeping. I had stopped going out for drinks on Friday nights with the guys. In fact, other than family dinners, I didn't get out much at all.

My roommate Charlie got sick of having me around all the time, so he convinced me I needed to find a hobby. I made an off-handed comment that I would like to try my hand at playing guitar. The guy spent hours a day on buy and sell websites, looking for what I was never really sure, but two days later he found one. It was a Japanese built Fender Jaguar. It looked to be in pretty good shape and the price was right. After pressure from Charlie and a few quick texts exchanged with the seller, I made an appointment to go check it out that night after work.

The address was for a small used book store on the west end. I got off the bus a few stops early to get some fresh air and ease my queasy stomach. The three blocks I walked gave me a chance to check out the neighbourhood. I scanned the windows of the antique stores and freshly renovated boutique shops. It had been a long time since I'd been down that way. It was nice to see things turning around.

The app on my phone told me I had arrived, so I stopped and turned toward the storefront. The name on the tattered canopy sign, from what I could see, looked right. The address on the door did too. I was about to step forward but paused to let a couple little old ladies pass by. One of them looked at me. She smiled and said hello. I smiled back. It was more of an automatic response than anything else. When they had gone on their way, I walked up, pulled on the wood door and then went inside. The jangle of bells overhead announced my arrival.

Dim light filtered through the blinds on the front window. Tight rows of mismatched shelves, stuffed to overflowing, ran from front to back. The front counter was to the left of the door with the cash register and other miscellaneous counter type stuff on top. It smelled exactly like I thought it would, aging paper and dust.

I was caught up in the old Dylan tune coming from the pair of small speakers hanging from the ceiling when someone called out from the back.

"Hey there, can I help you with anything?"

"Uh, yeah. I'm here to see Dale."

"Sure, hold tight a minute."

3

Something I do when I'm waiting to meet someone for the first time is to try and figure out what they're going to look like, maybe how they talk, or their mannerisms. I didn't have much to go on really. A name, and a few words on my phone screen. My expectations rarely match the reality, but I had never been so wrong as when Dale came around a pile of forgotten words bound by paper and glue.

"Hey, I'm Dale."

I froze when I looked down at the hand being extended toward me. Before I had a chance to check myself I said it, all of my innate awkwardness was put into four simple words: "But you're a woman?"

She tilted her head. "Last time I looked I have all the right parts, yeah."

Being the charmer I am, I just stood there and stared. It was hard not to.

She watched me through the thick black frames of her glasses. Her eyes were a deep emerald green like you see in pristine mountain lakes. Her jet black hair was tied back haphazardly and revealed a fair complexion. The small diamond piercing on the left side of her upper lip and the tattoo peeking out of her wide v-neck sweater hinted that she wasn't typical of the women I tended to associate with. The mischievous look on her face confirmed it.

"Let's try this again." The words came slow and she enunciated each one. "Hi there, my name is Dale. You are?"

I could feel the flush in my cheeks. "Sorry, I'm Adrian. I'm here for the guitar." Not knowing what else to do, I stuck out my hand. "Nice to meet you." Dale grasped it and shook it once with feeling.

"Better," she said, and turned away. "Follow me, please."

Dale walked down the long row toward the back of the store. At the end she stopped to right a book that had fallen out of place, and then turned back toward me. "Are you coming?"

"Oh. Yeah, sorry."

I heard her snicker to herself and then she disappeared. I followed along, moving fast to try and catch up. I rounded a corner and saw a small door propped open along the back wall. An 'Employees Only' sign hung on it. Bright light, relative to the gloom of the rest of the store, flooded out. I poked my head in. The cluttered space held all manner of interesting items. A wire-framed mannequin bust, an old yellow mop bucket full of stale water, and shockingly enough, boxes of books.

"Here it is," Dale said, and held the guitar out to me.

I supported it with one hand flat on the back of the neck and one on the lower bout. I think I was afraid I would hurt it or something. The Olympic White finish showed better in person. The hardware and tortoise shell pick guard had just the right

5

amount of wear, for my taste anyway. It had been used, but not abused. In that moment, I fell in love for the second time in as many minutes.

"My old roommate left it behind," she said. "I really only play acoustic and there's bills to pay, right? Like I said, there shouldn't be any issues. He played it every now and then and it sounded really good."

I strummed the strings a few times, trying to make it look like I knew what I was doing. "She's beautiful," I said.

"So, you want it then?"

"Yeah, I do." I set the end of the guitar down between my feet and rested the neck against my leg. I reached into my left front pocket and pulled out a folded envelope full of twenties and fifties. I had intended on trying to get a bit of a better deal, but all of that went out the window pretty quick.

I handed the envelope to Dale with a strained smile. "I counted it twice, but you might want to check it just to be safe."

"I'm sure it's fine, you've got an honest face." She slipped the envelope into her back pocket. "Besides, I can find you if I need to. I know people."

I can only imagine the look on my face. It felt like every drop of blood in my body had drained to my toes.

Dale laughed. "It was a joke, hon." She checked her watch. "Listen, I need to close up. If you have any issues, you let me know, okay?"

"I appreciate it, thanks again."

We walked up to the front of the store together. Dale leaned back against the counter and crossed her arms. I gave a little wave with my free hand. "Have a good night."

Dale smiled."You too, Adrian."

That almost did me in. My head was swimming. I almost toppled a stack of sci-fi novels as I fumbled my way to the door. "Sorry," I said.

"It's all good. Take care."

"You too."

Before the door closed, I got one last look at those perfect green eyes. I took a deep breath in an attempt to pull myself together, and then I wandered off to find the nearest bus stop.

There's a lot I don't remember about that time. One day blended into another. Thing is, if I close my eyes, I can picture every detail of that night. The way the driver was hunched over the wheel when I got on the bus home. How the light slanted through the windows as the sun began to set. I can still feel the breeze on my face as I walked the last leg home, and how my heart danced like it was about to break free from my chest.

Sometimes people ask me, when did things change? How did I turn it all around? For me, there are few clear answers in life, but in this I'm confident. I tell them it was a Thursday. It was warm for being so late in the fall. And all it took was a small step in a new direction.

Smile

I'm sitting here thinking about cancer. I've decided that life isn't fair.

Celebrities get shout outs and hashtags, while our friends and family are taken from us and nobody knows. Everyone is talented. Everyone is important. Right?

I'm lost in thought, when the boy pops up in front of me. He's grinning from ear to ear, tongue sticking through the space where a tooth used to be.

"Hi, Dad."

Just as quick, he disappears. I realize that maybe I've got it all wrong. It's not about recognition, it's what we do with the time we are given that counts.

I check my watch for what must be the tenth time. I'm not sure where Allison is but I hope to hell she shows up soon. Not that it's an unpleasant day. The sky is overcast, but calm. The temperature is just right. I don't like waiting, that's all.

I'm sitting on a bench facing the main path. People-watching, I guess you could say. There's a large green space behind me filled with activity. Couples are chatting. Children are playing and making all sorts of annoying noises.

I'm distracted by a pair of long legs in a short skirt so I don't see the projectile coming at me until it's too late. I rub my temple with the palm of my hand, trying to massage the stinging sensation away. A memory from the past comes to me. I hear my mother's voice, something about a clout to the ear. A young kid comes running up to retrieve a small red and black ball from the ground in front of me.

"Sorry about that."

"Yeah, it's okay." Sure, I'm lying, but what am I supposed to say?

The kid is standing there staring at me. He's scrawny with a messy ginger mop hanging down into his freckled face. He's wearing shorts and a t-shirt with a cartoon T-Rex that says 'Rawr! means "I love you" in dinosaur'. The socks and sandals are a nice touch. He's got a weird sparkle in his eye, like he's a little touched. As soon as he opens his mouth I know I'm in trouble.

"Wanna know something cool? I have an owl collection. Snowy owls are my favourite. I have two stuffies, the bigger one is Snowy and the smaller one is Snowy Junior. My Grandpa has a real snowy owl on the wall of his basement, I haven't named him yet but I will one day. Did you know that snowy owls aren't all white? They have brown bars and spots on their backs, and the males are smaller than the females. Weird right? My Uncle Steve, he's my Mom's brother, but my Uncle, he went to Nunavut once and got me a little owl made of seal fur. It's called an ookpik, he says that's the word for snowy owl in some other language. I love snowy owls. Do you know that one time I was having a picnic in the living room with Snowy and Snowy Junior, and we were drinking Tang and we each had our own cups, but I knocked the pitcher over by accident. Everything was orange! Mom wasn't happy because her new couch and fuzzy carpet used to be white. Dad says that's what you get for having a white couch and fuzzy carpet, and then Mom got very quiet and they went upstairs to talk. They do that a lot. Did you know that..."

He keeps going. I feel like I've been sucked into a bad Abbot and Costello skit. At one point I think I even say 'Who's on first?' The kid doesn't seem to notice. I manage to break my attention away to see Allison scurrying up the path toward us.

She looks flustered. Flabbergasted even. I didn't know the word was in my vocabulary. Maybe the kid used it in one of his unlimited supply of obscure stories.

Allison stops in front of me and the kid's story trails off into silence. We're both rendered speechless by the vision standing before us. The world around her looks dull and uninteresting in comparison. She has that effect on people. I hate to admit it's something I take for granted every now and then, but it's good to be reminded how lucky I am.

"Hey, Dan. I'm so sorry, my roommate had a meltdown just as I was trying to leave and then the train was running behind because of some accident downtown…"

"It's okay, really."

Her eyes soften and she gives an embarrassed smile. The kid sniffles and wipes at his nose with the hem of his shirt. Allison looks down to the kid. "Who's this?"

"Oh, him? Just a friend. We were having a chat."

The kid's eyes light up and a big toothy grin fills his face. I stand and take Allison's hand in mine. Our eyes lock and all my cares fade away.

"Come on, let's go."

I turn back as we move away up the path. "See ya, kid. Good luck with your owls."

Thankful

"Where you headed?"

"Falls Church."

"What's taking you down there?"

"Family stuff. It's home. Used to be anyway."

"That so? Well, I've got a second cousin lives out that way, maybe you know her? Esme Whitmore?"

"Sorry, doesn't ring a bell."

"Really? She's run a dance school out there for years."

"Sorry."

"Well, that's alright, you been gone, I guess."

"Yeah."

"So, you're going to see family then?"

"I… Yes. My mother, she had an accident."

"Oh my. That's terrible. She gonna be alright?"

"Yeah. She will."

"Something to be thankful for at least."

"Yeah. I guess you're right."

Welcome Back

I walked in to find a note on my desk.

Hello love. Call me please.

I dropped to my seat and flipped my note book open. I grabbed the handset and held my finger over the buttons. The numbers didn't come to mind as easily as they used to. I held my breath as the digital tone sounded in my ear.

"Hey, you," she said.

"Good morning."

"Where've you been?"

"Away. I needed a bit of a break. It lasted a lot longer than I had hoped."

"Well, you're back now. That's what's important."

I smiled. "Yes it is."

Follow Your Dreams

I watch as she sits at the table in the corner. She pushes her hat back on her head, and then wraps both hands around the coffee cup in front of her.

I think about last night's dream.

We were sitting on a park bench. The sky was like amethyst. It smelled of rain.

I couldn't face her, so I stared at the bricks of the path in front of us. "I think I'm ready," I said.

"I've told you how it will end."

"I know. It will be worth it."

She leaned in and gave me a lingering kiss on the cheek. Our eyes met, she smiled at me, and the dream faded.

I take a deep breath, stand, and walk over to her table. My smile is awkward, I'm so nervous. She looks up at me and I'm taken back to the dream and I remember it all. My heartbeat settles, and the tension leaves my shoulders.

I take a step closer. "Hi, my name is Brandon. Would it be okay if I joined you?"

Sweat is dripping into my eyes. I lift the cloth from the edge of the tub and wipe my forehead and face. I can never seem to get the temperature of the water right. It's either too hot, or not hot enough. Now that I think about it, sounds like a lot of my relationships.

Now I'm thinking about you again. About that day last September when the thunder was rolling but the sun was still shining. We ran through the rain like a couple of stupid kids. Or the time we rode the trolley to the end of the line because we didn't want it to stop. When they made us get off, you bought us treats from the ice cream cart at the park. I leaned in for a kiss, and my popsicle dripped on your dress. You smiled and said it was okay. In that moment, I think I finally understood what love is.

I'm so full of irrational fears. They're a constant loop in my brain. I worry about how to beat the odds when you only have a fifty percent chance. I wonder why you love me, what it is that you see in me. Sometimes I worry I don't have the courage to love you the way that I want to. If I put it all down on paper, could I make you understand? When is the last time I wrote an actual letter? I stare at my hands. They're wrinkled and pale. I wonder if I could still hold a pen when they look like this.

The latch on the door clicks and it eases open.

"Hey, I just wanted to let you know I was home."

I sit up and turn toward you. "Hi. I'm almost done, I'll be down soon."

"Okay." You smile. Your lips shine almost as bright as your eyes.

My chest tingles and my face is flush with warmth. The door closes and my shoulders dip back below the surface. I draw in a deep breath, and then reach down to pull the plug. The water begins to drain away, and with it, go all of my worries.

THAT

Mary

Mary woke that early summer morning to the warmth of the sun on her face and the sound of sparrows chattering in the distance. She sat up in bed, shielding her eyes against the light, and knew that it was going to be a special day. After dressing and fixing a cup of black coffee and a piece of toast for breakfast, she decided to tidy the house.

Mary slid open the window above the kitchen sink and then grabbed a feather duster from the cupboard below. She shuffled into the living room, dusted her small collection of ceramic figurines, and then the cluster of family photos hanging on the south wall. Mary gave only brief glances to the faces from the past as the feathers wiped clean their wood framed enclosures. She paused at one though, brought her frail fingers to her lips, and then held them against the glass. Beneath her touch was her husband Harold, standing tall in his khaki battle dress a short time before being deployed.

The past three years had been a trying time for Mary, as anyone who had lost the love of their life after sixty-six years of marriage could attest to. No one would have imagined that Harold, who had been through so much in his life, would be run down by the 3:30 bus as it made its way downtown on an otherwise pleasant spring day.

It wasn't that Mary was alone. Family members in the area would stop by to drop off groceries or check on the house, but mostly to make sure that she hadn't gone crazy and started collecting cats. Mary's next door neighbour Brenda would stop by once a week with a care package, sometimes a small casserole, but more often a sweet snack. While Mary appreciated the gestures, she felt there was something vital missing from her life.

Once Mary had finished in the living room, she focused her attention on the bedroom. While clearing out various boxes and bags from the closet, she found one of Harold's socks stuck in between an old suitcase and the back wall.

Mary sat on the edge of her bed, staring at the sock in her hand. A fresh sense of loss overtook her. Memories of the life they had built together came to her mind like scenes from an old movie projector. Soon, a wonderful thought took root. As it grew, so did the first genuine smile Mary had known since Harold passed.

She stood and made her way to the basement and then into the laundry room. In one corner was her sewing machine, tucked away in its table. On the wall was a cupboard which Harold had built to store her sewing supplies. From the cupboard Mary retrieved her fold out sewing box and a small plastic container. She placed them on top of the sewing table along with Harold's sock. Mary pulled out a stool from under the sewing machine and sat down on the cold vinyl seat. She took out a packet of needles and a half-used spool of thread from the sewing kit, and then set the sock on the center of the table to consider her next step.

To the casual observer the sock itself was nothing special. The elastic at the cuff was beginning to show, the plain black fabric was fading and thinning at the heel.

Mary removed the lid from the Tupperware container, and pushed a finger through the contents until she found and removed two large jade buttons. Those particular buttons had come from a rain coat that Harold had given her on her fiftieth birthday. It had been ruined after being caught in the door of Harold's 1976 Buick Electra. Mary had always disliked that car, even more so after the incident. She was not able to mend the tear, but had kept the buttons as a memento.

Mary fought the tremors in her hands as she wove the needle and thread through the fabric of the sock. After a few minutes of creative stitching and the addition of the jade buttons, she deemed the project complete. She turned the sock over, inspecting her work. She grabbed the cuff and without hesitation, slipped her free hand inside. That was when Martin came to life.

It would be easy to dismiss Martin for the simple fact that he was a sock puppet, but to Mary he was so much more. Martin was charismatic, funny, and most important of all, a good listener. Mary was so happy to have someone to share her life with again.

Every day for tea, Mary would set out a china tea set on a freshly polished silver platter. Her Aunt Ruby had purchased the ornate jasperware tea pot with matching cups and saucers while visiting family in England. She had given them to Mary and Harold as a housewarming gift. Mary was very proud of the set and only used it on special occasions. One of the cups had a small chip in its soft blue finish. Mary used it to hold a few fresh-cut gardenias taken from the planters that her niece Jessica had brought to brighten up the front steps. After tea they would often play a hand or two of bridge. Being the gentleman he was, Martin would often let Mary win.

In the evenings they would relax out on the veranda, swaying away the hours in an old rocking chair. On occasion, they would even stay out to watch the sun set. Mary's neighbours remarked how nice it was to have her out and about again, even if they were somewhat concerned that she was not to be seen without a sock on her hand.

One night, after enjoying a particularly beautiful sunset, Mary retrieved a small box hidden in the back of her nightstand and retired to the living room. She sat down in one of the matching wingback chairs and placed the box on her lap. Between the chairs was an old Tiffany-style lamp atop a simple wooden side table. Mary reached under the white and green stained glass shade and pulled the chain. She sat in the dim light, staring at the box, her free hand caressing the plain wooden top. Not wanting to be rude, Martin waited in silence while Mary collected her thoughts.

When she was ready, Mary opened the box and removed the small bundle of letters that Harold had written her while he was away fighting in the war. One by one, she unfolded each letter and read them aloud to Martin. They described Harold's travels through Italy with the Princess Patricia's Canadian Light Infantry. Although he omitted many of the more terrible truths of the war, Mary could sense his sadness. At the end of every letter he expressed how much he missed her, and how in love he was with her.

Mary told Martin how proud she was of Harold, and how scared she was at the time that he might not return. Harold did come home late in October of 1945, and they were married a few short days later. She explained how from that moment until Harold was taken from her for good, they had not spent a single day apart.

Mary shared how difficult the past three years had been, waking up every morning without her soul mate beside her, adjusting to a life lived alone, and doing her best to hold on to the home where they had raised their children and grown old together. She told Martin how desperately she longed to see Harold again. Martin did his best to console Mary. He told her how brave she had been to carry on, but that now she could rest easy. Harold was waiting for her, and she would be seeing him again very soon.

*

Brenda stood huddled in her housecoat, watching out the window as thick, grey clouds were building to the north. She decided it would be a perfect day to make a fresh batch of strawberry scones, a particular favourite of Mary's, and to stop by for her weekly visit.

The scent of fresh baking began drifting through the house as the timer on the oven called out. Brenda donned one of the oven mitts that hung on the wall beside the stove and removed the golden brown scones from the oven. After allowing them to cool for a moment she divided them onto two separate plates. One she covered with a clean tea towel for the journey next door, the other she set on the kitchen table. She picked up the covered plate of scones and then was out the front door, pausing only to pull in the morning newspaper and toss it onto her husband's tattered old recliner.

Brenda made her way up the walkway and through the gate to Mary's back door. She knocked three times, and rang the bell, but there was no answer. Brenda was surprised when the

25

doorknob turned in her hand. She stepped into the porch and called out Mary's name.

The house was dark except for the dim glow of artificial light coming from the entrance to the living room. Brenda walked in to find the blinds drawn and an ornate lamp casting faint shadows throughout the room. She saw Mary sitting back in an oversized arm chair. Brenda spoke Mary's name, out of acknowledgement more so than any hope of a response.

Brenda stepped around an empty picture frame lying on the floor, and placed a hand on the cold porcelain skin of Mary's arm. Hand-written letters covered her lap and the exposed seat of the chair. Mary had a contented smile on her face. She was holding a picture of Harold close to her heart with her right hand. Her left hand, clad with an old sock, was resting against her cheek.

The Stag

The stag is standing there staring at me. I don't take my eyes off of him either. He only fades as wisps of my own breath rise and disintegrate in front of me. I'm too scared to move, not that there's anywhere for me to run.

"Git!" I shout at him. He doesn't move, only twitches his nose.

"Go on now!" Eyes as deep and dark as an empty well are locked on me, waiting. "Beat it, ya wretch!"

I shift my stance to ease the pain in my foot. The stag levels his head at me and takes a single step forward. I feel warmth running down my leg as I drop to my knees and start to pray.

Dreaming in Circles

I opened my eyes to find myself standing in a barren wasteland of ice and snow. The sun was in the process of rising but at the same time did not appear to be making any progress. The world shifted in an odd way, like I was standing at the pivot of a merry-go-round.

I don't know how I knew, whether through some unnatural ability or the actual sense of the globe spinning, but it occurred to me that I was standing at geographical north. Where I half expected to see a red and white striped pole, an old Inuit woman was sitting atop a mound of ice and snow.

She wore a long caribou parka. The wide hood was pushed back exposing silver hair tied tight against her head and a weathered face like old leather. I couldn't see her eyes, only the creases where they should have been. Below her flat nose was a broad smile of amusement and welcome. I raised a hand to the old woman. She sat with her hands in her lap and didn't respond.

It was at that point that my attention was drawn to slow movement in my peripheral. I turned to my right and saw a polar bear approaching. I froze as his dark eyes fixed on me. He was a monster, at least twice my height if he had stood upright. The fur along his back glowed with a yellow and orange halo in the light of the rising sun.

I managed to keep control over my bowels as the bear resumed his slow pace toward me. I took a few steps back. The bear increased his pace. I turned and sprinted around the old woman on the mound. The bear stayed close behind, his shadow would envelope me and then abate. Again and again. Round and round.

"Six o'clock! Five o'clock! Four o'clock!" The old Inuit woman cackled, "Run, time traveler!"

I kept running in circles, sensing the imaginary time zones fly past. The old woman laughed like it was the best thing she'd seen in years. She kicked her seal skin boots against the ice in glee. At one point she was laughing so hard that she began to cough and convulse, almost tumbling off of her perch.

Three days into the past my legs were burning. The bear's massive paws pounded the ice behind me, closer with every step. I felt breath on the back of my neck and then a sharp pain on my right side. My body folded and everything went dark.

When I opened my eyes I was lying on the simulated hardwood of my bedroom floor. Out of breath, I crawled back into bed and tried to calm my racing heart as the sights and sounds of the dream echoed in my mind.

Boots

"Get the gun outta my face!"

The stranger shifted in place. "I said give me your boots, man." One eye was almost swollen shut. His free hand was against his torso. Blood had soaked into the material of his shirt and was dripping between his fingers. The cuffs of his jeans were damp. His feet were scratched and raw at the soles. The pinky toe on his left foot was missing the nail.

"Listen, I don't want any trouble."

The man steadied the revolver and pulled the hammer back. "Take 'em off and walk away, won't be no trouble."

The Last Trip

The old man shuffled through a skiff of fresh snow toward the barn. The full moon was high in the now cloudless sky, lighting the way. He held the front of his tattered overcoat closed with one hand, the other was buried in a side pocket. The vapour from his breath fogged his round spectacles, but it did little to hinder his advance.

He stopped in front of the barn door and fumbled with the latch. He strained to push the door on its slide. It locked open with a dull clunk. The old man paused and turned to look back at the house. A thin wisp of smoke came from the chimney above. A single frosted window was alight with a gentle glow.

It hadn't been an easy conversation. The old man's wife had been supportive for many years, but she was less than thrilled with the news that he was planning on heading out that night. He promised her it would be the last time. She pointed out that the promise had been made before. This time was different he had said. She said nothing more.

The old man turned back to the barn. The cutter was sitting in the light of a moon beam. It had been his first. Now it was an antique, held together with little more than a few stray nails and faith. He walked past empty stable stalls, six in all, and laid a shaking hand on the simple curved dash of the sleigh. So many wonderful memories. He looked to his hand, pale and arthritic, and wondered where the time had gone. A lot had changed since the old girl had been out last. In fact, he had a hard time remembering a single thing that was the same.

The old man turned at the scraping of hooves beside him. He walked to the last of the stalls. Standing near each of the stable gates were two great caribou. Sinewy muscles flexed beneath glossy coats. Their large ornate antlers bobbed with the motion of their heads. The old man spread his hands out, scratching at their chins. They were the last, the only ones who had stayed.

The old man put his hands in his pockets and looked to the harnesses on the wall. No words were spoken. None were needed. This would be the last trip, whether he liked it or not.

Isolation

The jaguar hasn't moved in a while. Neither have I. Every now and then he flicks an ear on his broad head, or blinks in a way to suggest that I'm of no real interest. Still his eyes stay focused on me, and my eyes stay focused on him.

   We seem to share some sort of connection, though it isn't from any sense of being alike. This magnificent beast, once wild and without equal, sits humiliated in his cramped concrete enclosure. I stand before him, alone in a room full of people, lost in what I'm told is freedom.

Sunday Morning

Jimmy Bones stumbled through the front door of his mother's apartment. He held one hand against the wall as he made his way to the kitchen to find something to drink that didn't contain alcohol. It had been a long night. Nine Toes Jenny had an appetite for trouble and Jimmy couldn't help but follow along. Maybe one day he would realize that she wasn't worth the trouble. Maybe.

He paused as he reached the edge of the kitchen table. Something was off, but the booze, pills, and God knows what else he had ingested over the last twenty-four hours were preventing his few remaining brain cells from making the connection. On the other side of the kitchen table sat an old, chipped side plate with a half-finished cigarette hanging on the rim. Lazy smoke drifted up to the ceiling, undisturbed. A single high backed chair sat at an odd angle away from the table. Looking down he saw his mother's bare feet, cracked and calloused, sticking out from underneath the table.

"Ma!"

Jimmy ran around the kitchen table to see his mother sprawled out on the floor. Her tattered floral night gown covered her like a drop sheet at a crime scene. Her eyelids fluttered as she regained consciousness.

"Jesus Ma, ya fainted again, d'int ya?"

Jimmy's mother muttered something unintelligible as Jimmy fought to haul her frail body upright.

"Come on, let's get ya to the window, the fresh air'll be good for ya."

When Jimmy got her upright, she spun away from him and back toward her spot at the table.

"Don't, Ma!"

"I need my smoke, boy!"

"Ma, ya need to get some air!"

"Dammit, I ain't gonna faint no more, let me get my smoke."

Jimmy's mother had one hand flat on the table top, Jimmy held her under her other arm. She reached out and snatched the lit cigarette from the plate and then set it in the corner of her mouth.

"Alright, let's get me some air then."

Scatter My Ashes Over Fields of Gold

Behind the main house there's an old wooden bench. It's just past a row of spruce trees and faces out over the fields and rolling hills that mark the edge of our property on the southeast side. My wife is sitting in her usual spot. I join her, in much the same way I have countless times before. We don't speak, but enjoy the last of the sun's warmth as it begins to fade over the horizon.

A cool breeze is pushing in from the north. We listen as it weaves through the trees and the open fields. A yellow-headed blackbird flies past in a silent arc toward the west.

Footsteps along the narrow pathway behind us announce the arrival of our guests. Many of our family and friends are here. Some brought campers or have driven in from one of the motels in town, but many have been staying in the cabins off of the north road. It's nice to see them in use again. I haven't paid much attention to them since we shut down the retreat a few years ago.

I see my children, grandchildren, and great grandchildren. Some are too young to understand what is happening I'm sure. I make special note of those that couldn't be here, whether by their own choosing or not. I'm grateful to all those who could make it. It's not often that you can get four generations of family together. But then, this is a special occasion.

Groups of people gather on either side of the wooden bench. There is much holding of hands and thin-lipped smiles that hold no joy. No words are spoken above a whisper. It's hard to know what to say. I've certainly been through this type of situation enough to know.

People come forward to say a few nice words. Some share a funny story or two. Memories from a time long ago. It's nice to hear laughter, to see everyone experience a moment of joy, fleeting though it may be.

After the last person has finished, our youngest grand-daughter moves in front of the crowd. In one hand she has a small stool, in the other one of my old guitars. She sits without speaking and begins to play.

The first chords ring out and I feel great warmth in my heart. Our granddaughter is playing her own composition. I'm so proud of her. She's so young but already following her dreams. We've been lucky that many of our family have had the courage to do the same.

I turn to my wife. She continues to look forward, watching the fields sway and the sun set. I see the sadness in her eyes. It hurts me so much to see her like this. I look down toward her hands, folded on her lap. I want to reach out, but I don't.

"Well, dear, I didn't quite make it to a hundred and three like I had hoped." I smile a little at my own inside joke, even though it does little to lighten the mood. "It's been a tough couple of weeks to say the least. For all of you of course, but for me too. Watching the people I love suffer like this. I especially never wanted you to hurt this way. Leaving you is going to be the hardest thing I've ever done."

My emotions are getting the best of me. I stop to look out over the fields again and listen for a while.

"The actual passing wasn't so bad. Nothing like I expected. Not that I had any expectations really. When it's time, don't be afraid."

The music ends with a few gentle notes. Among the shuffling feet and sniffling noses, everyone turns their attention to the old wooden bench. My wife, framed by the spruce trees, turns to her right and reaches for the simple urn beside her. The boys come forward and help her to stand.

Her body is frail, her skin sagging. Still, I see the strong, beautiful woman I married so many years ago. Together they walk forward to the edge of the field. I follow a few short paces behind.

There is a pause for a silent prayer as the last rays of the fading sun radiate over what seems to be unending prairie. My wife removes the lid from the urn and passes it to our firstborn. With a series of strained motions she tosses my ashes to be

38

carried on the breeze over our fields of gold. I reach out in a vain attempt to brush the tears streaking her cheek, hoping in some way that she knows I am close.

"It was perfect," I say, "thank you." I close my eyes, fighting back tears myself. "I love you," I say, and then it all fades away.

Listless

"Hey, wake up."

"Hmm?"

"Wake up, we have to go."

"What? Where?"

"We're meeting my mother for dinner, remember?"

"Oh. Right."

"Let's go, we're going to be late."

"Jesus, give me a minute, would ya?"

"Okay, cranky pants, calm down. That was your second nap today, are you feeling alright?"

"I think so. Not sure."

"Not sure? What does that mean?"

"It means I'm not sure. What do you want me to say?"

"I don't know. Maybe you should figure it out though."

"Yeah, well, there's a lot to figure out I guess."

"Well then, what are you waiting for?"

The Ride

I had a dream last night.

I was riding shotgun in an old Volkswagen Kombi. The headlights showed little of the landscape as we barreled down a narrow dirt road in the desolate wilds of Australia. There were so many stars in the clear night sky that I couldn't pick out anything familiar.

The inside of the Kombi was dusty but uncluttered. It smelled faintly of salt water. The passenger compartment held only a large canvas bag and a pile of wrinkled clothes. A small cluster of foam floats sat in the bunt of a throw net hanging along the driver's side back window. The AM radio couldn't pick up a signal, or it was broken, I don't remember.

The flatulent Aboriginal behind the wheel wasn't much for conversation. He was hunched forward, forearms resting on the steering wheel. Every now and then he would brush the unkempt mop of silver streaked wavy hair out of his eyes. His bushy white beard seemed to have secrets of its own. Above the waist he was naked except for a thin rope necklace with a clutch of quills hanging low. His dark skin glistened in the dim glow of the instrument cluster.

He noticed my judgmental glance after the textbook definition of 'silent but deadly' enveloped the cabin. His wide smile showed all of his remaining teeth, yellow and crooked. "Powered by natural gas, mate."

Without taking his eyes off of the road he reached down into a brown paper bag sitting between the front seats and brought up half a sandwich. He looked at me, offering the wedge in my direction. Between two pale white slices were what looked to be a thick cut piece of cheddar surrounded by a foul-smelling brown paste. After I declined he shrugged and bit off half of the sandwich in one go. He returned to his position at the wheel and chewed at the lump in his cheek.

We drove on in silence, save for the hum of the engine ticking away behind us. The empty turtle shell hanging from the rearview mirror swayed back and forth as we traversed uneven sections of the road.

After a time, my nameless friend pulled the Kombi over to the side of the road and turned the ignition off. "Need a rest." I asked him if we could keep going, just a little longer. "Nah mate, I'm buggered." With that he opened his door, hopped down to the dusty road, and then wandered off into the night. I crossed my arms and leaned back in my seat. I looked out into the dark. I sensed something moving just out of reach of the headlight. A wave of anxiety washed over me and it shook me from my dream.

I didn't sleep for the rest of the night. I still can't shake the feeling that something was waiting for me out in the dark.

What I don't know is if it's something to regret, or something that I should be grateful didn't find me.

The Meaning of Life is Written in the Stars

I don't understand how I keep getting myself into these situations. Clinton convinced me to come along to a weekend festival out in the middle of the Nevada desert. Said it would be great, lots of free-thinking, good-looking people expanding their minds. Damn him and his inability to do anything by himself.

We left the car in Henderson at about five in the morning. From there we were herded onto a retired school bus that had been converted to run off of used vegetable oil and had Precious Rebirth Spiritual Retreat hand painted on the side. After two hours of sitting on broken seat springs breathing in the faint odour of stale french fries, we were deposited at the festival site. Vibrantly decorated stages and large tents set up in the main area, a few camp sites and various forms of free accommodation were to the west.

It was a long day. We attended a number of seminars and workshops on pretty much every form of spiritual advancement you could imagine. Some were interesting, some were just plain crazy. So were most of the people attending. It seemed like I might have been the only one in the crowd who was wearing store-bought clothes or enjoyed the benefits of deodorant. I'd never experienced anything like it in my life.

After grabbing some dinner and wandering around the meager marketplace, Clinton had gone to sleep off the day's

44

adventures in an igloo made out of recycled phone books and hemp. I wasn't tired, so I set up shop at one of the bonfires just south of the camp. People came and went but I didn't take much notice, I was enjoying the sunset and the cool breeze coming in off of the dunes.

At one point, I looked up to find myself alone except for a rather large fellow who smelled vaguely of incense and cabbage. His rotund mass was not flattered by the large patchwork muumuu that adorned it. Beneath the long strands of greasy black hair were eyes devoid of any real emotion, no matter how wide the crooked but ever present smile on his face grew, and a nose best described as porcine in nature, flat and upturned.

He called himself Master Suraj, a self-proclaimed spiritual guru from Biloxi, who said that all the world's problems could be solved by embracing ISHTA yoga and self-love. I had seen him at a round table earlier in the day, he had come off as a bit of a flake and our meeting did nothing to improve on that impression.

He had an amazing talent for carrying a conversation all on his own. I couldn't have said more than ten words the whole time, but he just kept going. He shared his hypothesis of how man had evolved from an ancient race of half gods originally from a planet on the northern tip of the constellation Perseus. At some point he segued into describing the benefits of a juice cleanse that he had invented and patented. He explained that only a select variety of fruits and vegetables could be consumed, in very specific concentrations of course, and how it had done wonders for him personally. That might have been the one thing that I believed came out of his mouth, if by fruits and vegetables he meant bacon and chocolate cake.

It seemed like he had been talking for hours when he announced that he needed to go off for a wee. Don't worry, he told me, I'll be right back. I still need to get your email address so I can sign you up for my newsletter he said. I nodded and smiled politely in return, but as soon as that fat bastard was out of sight, I bolted.

I wandered into the desert, homesick and alone, while the small collection of fires glowed in the distance. I suffered in the knowledge that I had no hope of escape from the madness until the french fry bus came to get us the next day. I tried to keep my mind on other things, knowing that you worry most about the things you can't do anything about. I laid back in the sand and looked to the stars, searching for the constellation Perseus, and pondering the meaning of life.

Rearview Mirror

I'm driving down an empty secondary road. Up ahead I see something lying in the opposite lane. As I get closer the form takes shape. It's a rearview mirror.

I wonder why someone wouldn't want to look back. Did they no longer want to remember the things they said that made a friend cry, or the act of a loved one who broke their heart? Maybe they were afraid of their past catching up with them? I tighten my grip on the wheel, focus my attention ahead, and wonder if that might be the worst thing of them all.

What We Can Do Without

I was sitting at a bar, my arms crossed and resting on the worn oak top. An empty beer glass was in front of me. The lights in the room were dim, the shadows deep. An old man was sitting two spots down from me. He was wearing a worn pair of jeans with a braided belt. His faded button down shirt was at least one size too big for him. Underneath the wiry silver beard, his face was lined and creased. His thinning hair was slicked back. He had his arms out in front of him, hands turning a stained coffee mug.

I looked back at the sound of coins dropping into the jukebox. The room filled with sound as George started to sing. He said I'll love you till I die. The steel guitar came in and I heard the click of heels on the rough wood floor walking to one of the booths on the other side of the room. The old man looked up at me only for a moment. His eyes were dark and held a sadness that made me uncomfortable. He lowered his head, and then started talking.

"I think a lot about what the world can do with less of. Maybe even do without. Ignorance, or complacency. Things that cause so much pain, but nobody takes them as seriously as they should. Seems all the world wants to grow smaller is the number of hours we sleep at night, the length of a young lady's skirt, or the balance in our bank account." The old man chewed at his bottom lip. He looked back over his shoulder away from me, and then turned back to focus on the mug, and on his bent and arthritic hands. He was silent for a while, maybe listening as George cried out, as the strings soared. I turned away, thinking he was done, but I was wrong.

"Certain things we don't get a choice in. They're taken from us, even though we still need them. Some people say there're lessons in the pain, but I'm tired of learning that way." The old man picked up the mug with his left hand and drained the contents. He set it down, pushed himself back from the bar and then set his feet on the floor. He reached into his pants pocket and left a few coins on the bar top. The song faded away and the room fell silent. The old man kept his eyes on the floor as he walked out the door and into the night.

Going Home

I had a dream last night.

I was sitting on an old wooden bench, the paint all but worn away, on the edge of a bare gravel parking lot. To my right was a chipped and rusted enamel sign with 'BUS STOP' printed in bold letters, sitting atop a steel pole welded onto an old car wheel. The afternoon sun was just beginning to fade. The light breeze did little to cut the heat of the day. A lone bird hidden in a nearby oak tree sang an unfamiliar tune.

Behind me across the lot was a small service station. The nondescript white box had a sign above the entrance that simply said 'Chuck's Service' and a red enamel Pegasus sign beside. Two service bays with glass paned doors sat off to the right. Two gas pumps were abandoned out front. A few people appeared to be milling about inside but they were indistinct through the shadows and small dusty windows.

I was watching the rutted two lane road in front of me when a young man sat down on the opposite end of the bench. He propped up a guitar case, the neck leaning against the seat close to his side. I nodded and smiled. He returned the gesture in kind.

The young man was in a clean tan suit with a dark printed tie and pressed white shirt. His shoes showed the dust and toil of a long journey. Clean shaven, his dark skin glistened in the fading sunlight. His black hair, shaved close on the sides, was slicked back in glossy waves up top. He exuded confidence and charm. He had no luggage, only the guitar. Like everything else around me, he seemed to be from a time long gone.

The young man reached up with a silk handkerchief to wipe the perspiration from his brow and caught me staring at the case beside him.

"You play?"

"I try," I said. "It's hard to find the time to keep it up, though."

He spoke in a slow, comfortable drawl. "Yeah, life gets busier every day. It's all about choosing how you want to spend your time, I suppose."

I'm not sure why I chose to open up to him, but I did.

"Making that choice is the hardest thing. I get scared sometimes. I feel lost, like I'm living someone else's life. I don't know how to get where I want to be."

"Well, we all struggle inside. The point is to do the best you can. Make a difference to as many people as you can."

"I just feel like I've wasted so much time."

"Then do whatever you have to do to be happy now. It's never too late to change direction. There's no point in wasting your time with regrets."

I smiled. "Pretty wise words coming from someone so young."

He smiled back and looked down at the ground. "Oh, I've been through enough. But I don't feel bad." He looked up into the cloudless sky. "I'm finally going home."

I followed his gaze. We both sat in silence, watching nothing in particular, until the clatter of a large internal combustion engine broke the trance. In a flurry of noise and billowing clouds of dust, an old Continental Trailways bus swerved off the road and came to an abrupt stop in front of us. The door opened with an unpleasant groan.

The young man stood and picked up the guitar case in his left hand. "Well, I've got to go. It's been nice talking with you."

"It's been nice talking to you too." I stood and put my hand out. "Sorry, I should have introduced myself. My name is Shane."

His grip was firm. "Riley. Nice to make your acquaintance."

He gave a broad smile, nodded once, and then made his way up the steps into the waiting bus. I closed my eyes as the engine revved and it accelerated away, kicking up another cloud of dust.

When I opened them, the sun was fighting to make its way through mottled grey cloud cover. Outside my bedroom window rain was falling in a slow drizzle. A lone robin sang in the distance. I sat up in bed and I knew something was different, that something important had been lost forever.

THE OTHER

David sat alone on the park bench. The sun was high in the sky and the full heat of the afternoon just coming on. He adjusted his hat, and then turned the page of his book.

A man in a long tan trench coat walked along the path in front of David. He had dark, wavy hair that was slicked back on the sides. Wrinkles were starting to take hold around his eyes. He wore a look of contemplation. The man slowed and stopped a few steps past the bench. He seemed to look up at the birds in the trees, or maybe a passing cloud, but then moved back toward the bench and sat down.

"Beautiful day."

David didn't look up. "Yes, it is."

"Are you enjoying the book?"

"I am."

"Glad to hear. I think you'll find the ending quite interesting."

David gave a thin-lipped smile.

"I mean, the uncle? You just don't see it coming!"

David frowned and looked at the man from the corner of his eye. He laid the open book face down over his knee.

The man fumbled around the inside pocket of his coat and pulled out a tarnished silver cigarette case. He held it up. "Do you mind?"

"Actually I…"

The man lowered a cupped hand and blew smoke from the corner of his mouth. He held the smoldering cigarette pinched between his thumb and pointer finger.

David leaned away and held his breath as he waved smoke away from his face.

The man took a drag from his cigarette and pointed at the book on David's leg. "I quite enjoy the author. She has a way of making you comfortable, and then bam!" he clapped his free hand against his knee, "everything gets turned on its head."

David's eyes widened and he nodded with a slight frown on his face.

"The whole series is very popular I hear, have you read any of the others?"

"I have. This is the third."

"I'm sure you know this, but all of her books are set in and around medieval Scotland. Her descriptions are just wonderful, very accurate. The feel of it, you know? It's spooky. She must have done a great deal of research."

"I'm sure she did."

"Her father was also a writer. Delightful man. I met him once, a long time ago."

David pinched his eyebrows together. "But, didn't he die shortly after the war?"

"Did he? Oh, that is unfortunate news."

David watched the man's face. "I'm sorry, who are you exactly?"

"Oh, I'm glad you asked," the man smiled wide, "I am a genie."

"A genie? Like, the three wishes type?"

"Yes. Well, that's the basic idea anyway."

David looked around. "But where's your lamp?"

"I don't have one."

"Why not?"

"Not all stories have to be true all the time."

"Or maybe you're not really a genie?"

"Is that what you think?"

"Why wouldn't I? Genies aren't real."

"Oh? I'm very sorry to hear that." The man frowned. "Let's say, just for a moment, that you are wrong. Given the chance, what would you wish for?"

"I'm not sure. What do people normally wish for in these types of situations? You know, given the chance."

"Well," the genie said, crossing his arms and leaning back, "that is a very good question. For the most part they are the same. Love, or hate, or greed. The most basic of instincts I suppose. A lot of people ask for money. The problem with that is, once you get some, you generally want more. Perhaps that goes for most things though. Answer me this. Why are there billionaires? Who could ever need that much? I'll tell you, it comes down to power over others. Why else would it be necessary? One person could eliminate most of the world's poverty, but does it happen? Of course not." The man shook his head. "All that money, just sitting around. When they die it goes to their children, or their lawyers, and the cycle will repeat. How does that make any sense?"

"So is that why people ask for it? Just to be rich?"

"Some think it will give them freedom. From what? That is different each time. I never understood it, truth be told. Trust me, true freedom isn't something you would enjoy. We all need things to attach ourselves to. Not physical things mind you, but people, or ideals. These help define who you are. Anyway, most are just greedy, I suppose."

The man waved a finger. "Speaking of being greedy, asking for more wishes, that's a classic. It doesn't happen as often as you'd think these days. Usually it comes from the old, because they know the stories, or from the young, because they're good at getting what they want. It should be easy, right? Just ask for more. A hundred maybe, or a hundred thousand, or the largest number you can think of. Who wouldn't want to have so many second chances? If the first wish doesn't work out, you can try and fix it. I've always wondered, would anything ever get done? If you had so many opportunities to make things perfect, would there be anything else? All your time would be spent adjusting, going back to a single moment over and over. There

59

would be nothing else but the act of trying to make life the way you want it to be, but at the same time it's slipping through your fingers. Experiencing the good and the bad is what life is all about. You know, life is the journey, not the destination." The man took another drag from his cigarette. "Anyway, back to what I was saying. People ask, but in this case they don't get. The universe is generous, but only to a point, no matter what people believe. One opportunity to change the course of history is a gift that shouldn't be taken lightly. Sometimes you only get one chance, you'd better make it count."

The man flicked the stub of his cigarette out across the path. He leaned forward with his elbows on his knees. His hands were flat, palm to palm. "Wishing for love is another big one, possibly the oldest story there is. It rarely ends the way you think, though. If the person making the wish has any sense, any bit of humanity, they walk away once they realize what they've gotten themselves into. Sadly that's not always the case. See, for many it's not even love they're looking for. It's subservience. Whether it's from a single person, or of many, the reasons don't change much. People are looking for something or someone to fill the hole inside, that place where you're supposed to love and care for yourself. I never understood it, wanting something that isn't real, especially something that is so important. Some people aren't right in the head. Don't get me wrong, everything and everyone has their place. Can you imagine if all actors, writers, and artists were well balanced and of sound mind? Sometimes the damaged bring the most beautiful creations into this world. Very little would be the same without them." The man paused. He leaned back and stretched his arms out along the bench. "Listen, being famous isn't the issue. Wanting to be loved isn't either. Needing to be famous might be. Expecting your love to be reciprocated simply because it exists for you certainly is. This is where things can go very, very wrong."

"Hate is a common sentiment. I don't know that I'll ever understand your people's tendency for violence. It lives in all of you, some just hide it better than others. I mean, look at your history, everything you've accomplished is built on the blood of perceived enemies. I don't know if I really want to talk about it to be honest, it makes me sick to my stomach. If people would simply talk to each other once in a while, so many conflicts could be avoided. It won't happen though. Not on a large scale."

"You don't think so?"

"I really don't. I've seen too much to think otherwise. Granted, you could say that I mostly get the worst of people, but the worst is very bad. More than you know."

"What about world peace?"

The man laughed. "What about it?"

"Has anyone wished for it?"

"Oh, they have. But there's only so much a wish can do. Sure, you can make people forget, but human nature can't be swayed so easily. Even if it was possible, people don't think about the consequences. Whole economies are supported by war, or by preparing for it. Do you know how many people would be out of work? The whole system would crash. And religion! Don't get me started. You people need to have an enemy or something to be afraid of, otherwise what's the point of waking up every day? Conflict is what makes the world go round, don't ever doubt that."

"Has anyone ever asked to live forever?"

"Not as many as you would think. It may seem that the only goal for some is to extend their existence past a reasonable point, but in this respect I think most people get it. Sure, there are some interesting benefits. You get to see cultures change and grow. You watch as cities are built, destroyed, and then rebuilt over whatever is left. If you're paying attention you notice the patterns. Things are, what's the word... cyclical. People come together and push hatred and fear back into a dark corner. Then you watch them get complacent and turn their backs as the bad things take hold again. The form may not be the same, but the idea behind it is."

The man sat up straight and cupped his hands over one knee. "Your family, friends, and lovers all get old and die. Or they don't get to be old at all. Either way, you get to watch them diminish and suffer in terrible ways. You think it's bad, but the worst is yet to come. You know why? Because you get to do it all over again. And then a few more times after that. It gets old pretty quick, let me tell you. Stay away from people you say. Well, that only works for so long." The man brushed at something on his sleeve. He kept his gaze low. "Trust me on this one. It's not all it's cracked up to be."

"So why do things more often than not go bad?"

"I think the problem is that you ask for something that isn't earned. You haven't overcome anything to be worthy of it, or you never had the skills to deal with it in the first place. Look around you. Humans are such an entitled bunch, and it's for the most ridiculous things. Possessions or status. Striving every day for more. When you don't get what you want the response is anger. You lash out against the very thing you wanted. It's a terrible way to be, but it happens every day. When it's all said and done it turns out the same way these things always do. People get left behind. People get hurt."

The man paused. He looked away up the path, and then back to David. "Listen, don't get me wrong. There is good in the world, but for some reason most of you like to keep the happy parts locked away. You judge people, celebrate their failures, all so you can feel better about all the pointless, shitty things you don't want to give up. How can anyone be content living like that? It isn't my fault. I didn't make you this way."

The man looked up to the sky and let out a long exhale. "Look at me now. I'm sorry, I didn't mean to get so upset." He rubbed at his forehead. "Maybe it's time to take some time away. It's been far too long."

"If it's true that people tend to waste these opportunities, then what do you get out of it?"

The man frowned, "I haven't really thought about it to be honest. Well, maybe that's a lie. In the grand scheme of things I am just a tool. My purpose is not to judge." The man chewed on his lower lip. "If it's not my problem, then why do I worry about it so much?"

David picked up the book from his knee, closed the cover, and then set it down on the bench. "I think that you see the potential but have to stand by and watch us waste it time and time again. I've seen it many times myself. People go out of their way to make choices that are harmful to themselves and the people they love. Having to constantly deal with that disappointment, it must wear on you after a while. It would for most I imagine. We only have so much tolerance for these things, many people don't realize it's a limited resource."

The man smiled, but it was without joy. "You are a wise man, my friend. Very wise."

"I don't know about that." David shifted in his spot, turning to face the man. "I like to observe, and to understand. I'd like to thank you for sharing your experiences, and your frustrations. To be honest, I already knew what I was going to wish for, but now I'm confident that I've made the right decision."

The man squinted at David. "You say you already knew, but I thought you didn't believe?"

"Oh." David smiled. "I believe. In fact, I've been trying to find you for years now. I first heard the stories when I was young. I say stories, because that's what most people think they are. I knew one day I would meet you, and now I have."

The genie smirked and spread his arms wide. "Well, here I am. What is your wish then?"

David clasped his hands together on his lap and stared straight ahead. "My wish is to leave this world when and how I choose. It may be selfish, but I don't want to suffer. I don't want to waste away in a cramped room that only smells of peroxide. I like to think I've done what I can to live a life of dignity, and it doesn't seem much to ask that I die the same way."

The genie tilted his head. "Do you really believe it's not much to ask?"

David shrugged. "Maybe it is, but I don't think it should be."

"That is your wish then?"

David looked to the genie. "Yes, it is."

The genie blinked. David saw a flash of colour in his eyes, like the last supernova in a dark universe.

The genie rested a hand on David's shoulder. "If it means anything, I believe you have chosen well." The genie stood, straightened his coat, and then walked away.

Promises

Never again, you said. You shouldn't make promises, I said.

What's tomorrow going to bring? There's no way to know until it comes, but for us it's usually not something to look forward to. I thought things had changed. I guess I was wrong. When I look into your eyes and see the uncertainty and the fear, I can't help but feel we've been here too many times before.

Never again, you said. But then here I am, and there you are. If we make it out of this alive, maybe never again should be more than a promise.

Into the Darkness

It was a dark and stormy night.

No, wait.

I mean, that's how these things normally start, right? Really, it was a bit breezy. I remember the moon was two days past full. That's called waning gibbous. My cousin Billy taught me that. I don't know, maybe it would have been better if it was all miserable, but it really wasn't that bad.

Sorry, where was I going with this? Oh, right. I was trying to, you know, set the scene. We decided to spend the weekend camping. Bo was with Nicole, and Darin came with his girl Morgan. Felix was on his own, the on-again off-again thing he had with Cecily was very off at the time. Me? I like to keep my options open, so I was flying solo too.

It wasn't out in the wilderness or anything. Bo's Grandma had some land, we only really went far enough out so we couldn't see the lights in the yard anymore. We found this nice little clearing with trees all around and a slow creek nearby. It was warm for being so late in the summer. Everything was still green, you could tell it wouldn't last much longer though.

Felix wandered around looking for a place he could bed down while the rest of us set up camp. Dumbass only brought a sleeping bag, no tent, not even a tarp. When he got back he told us he found what was left of an old log cabin. Bo said the original homestead was near where we were at, but it had been abandoned for, like, a hundred years or something. He said some bad stuff went on, that's why they left it all and started over down the way where his Grandma still was. Felix showed us some weird rocks he found, they had symbols and stuff carved into them. He pulled one out of his pocket and tossed it to me. It looked like something you'd see in a museum, or on one of those treasure hunter shows. I remember it made me feel weird so I gave it back to him right away. Funny thing is, once we started looking around we spotted a whole bunch of them.

Anyway, after the tents and such were up, we settled in. Bo started telling his stories, and we all had a couple drinks. Before I knew it the sun was going down. Clouds were drifting in and the whole sky was lit up orange and red. Felix said he needed to take a leak so he took off into the trees. Bo and Darin talked about their plans to go riding the week after. The girls started to talk about girl stuff. I just sat and watched the fire while I nursed my beer.

I was looking up at a bird flying off toward the horizon when I first heard the noise back in the trees. A twig snapped, then it sounded like some dead leaves shuffled around. We all turned to see what it might be. Nicole called out to Felix, told him to stop being stupid, that we weren't buying it. Felix didn't answer, and we didn't hear any more noise for a bit. Nicole already looked nervous, but when Felix jumped out from behind an old stump, she screamed like the devil himself was after her. The rest of us had a good laugh, but Nicole sure wasn't impressed. Felix was bent over, nearly crying. He stood and was wiping at his eyes when something moved in the shadows behind him and he pitched forward flat on the ground.

When he got up he looked kinda stunned, had dirt all up one side of his face. Everyone was laughing again, I was too, but not so hard I didn't see his eyes change. They went black, like the pupil covered his whole eyeball. Then he just sort of lifted off the ground. No shit, he was floating like one of those magicians, except without the bad camera angle. Things got quiet, the wind died down even. I remember the tree branches behind him settling. Nobody moved, except for Bo who flinched when he dropped his beer.

We all sat there staring for a minute, then Felix started talking. Well, I guess it sort of sounded like Felix, if he'd had a two pack a day habit since kindergarten. He said stuff about us, things he said was gonna happen one day.

Felix told Bo that sometime after he and Nicole get married that he'd lose his job at the mill and take up drinking. Told Nicole that she'd get good at telling people that she was clumsy. Fell down the stairs a lot, stuff like that. Said she wouldn't try to leave until after he started hitting their son too.

Next he looked at Darin. Said the secrets would get to him, eat him up inside until there was nothing left. Felix told him that he would die, lonely and afraid. Not alone, but lonely. At the time I thought that was weird. Darin just stared at Felix, right? I could almost hear his teeth grinding together. Felix wasn't done though, he pointed at Morgan next. Said she was hiding things too, and a lot worse was gonna come from that.

Last he looked at me, all deadpan like. Told me I was gonna turn out just like my daddy. I said, I never knew the man. He squinted those dark eyes at me and got a little half smile. All he said was, I know.

About that time Nicole blew her stack, started calling Felix names and telling him to knock it off. Well, he just hung there, watching her with those black eyes. Bo got tense, stood up and told Felix that he'd better stop it or he was going to have a problem. Well, that maybe wasn't the best move. Felix leaned forward, still floating in the air, and put his hands on his knees. He looked right at Bo with this big stupid grin on his face. You don't scare me, child, he said, even if you understood the power you have it would do you no good.

After that, Felix leaned back and spread his arms out. He laughed hard, except it wasn't like Felix at all anymore. It was thin, sounded like it was far off. Then his body went limp and he dropped. One ankle was a little crooked when he landed. We all heard the snap. Nobody moved at first, it took a minute for us to come back to reality. Bo ran off to call an ambulance. Darin and me got under Felix and walked him out while the girls put the fire out.

That was the last time we all hung out like that. Nobody talked about what happened. We all just dealt with it as best we could all on our own I guess.

Felix never did heal right. Not on the outside, I guess not on the inside either. After the cast came off he walked with a bit of a limp, but he didn't like people making a fuss about it. One night we were out drinking and I asked him about that night. He said he didn't remember a damned thing, then he changed the subject. He was different though, you know? He drank more than he used to, didn't smile near as much. I wish he'd have talked to me. Not sure how, but maybe I could've helped him. I think about it, usually in the middle of the night when I can't sleep. I wonder what that thing said to Felix in his own head. What it told him he could expect, or maybe, what it offered him. Then at least we could all know why he went back to that clearing all those months later. I only heard about it, but they said he took a bunch of those rocks with the symbols, made a big circle of 'em. Then he found a sturdy branch on one of the bigger trees and hung himself from it.

Bo and Nicole stuck it out, if only to prove the whole thing was a joke. They even got married last summer. It was nice as far as those things go. I haven't talked to them since. I did see Nicole's sister at the bar the other night. She told me that

Nicole's pregnant, and the whole family's really excited. Said it's gonna be a boy.

Darin and Morgan broke up a few months after. Maybe drifted apart is a better way to put it. They started keeping their own schedules, hanging out with different crowds. You know how that goes. Maybe the secrets got too much to bear. Maybe what came to light didn't do as much good as they hoped. Morgan moved out of town first. I'm still not sure where she went. Sometime after Darin moved to the city. We used to talk once or twice a year, just shootin' the shit mostly. That changed last week. I got home from work and there was a message on the machine. He was mad. Said we needed to talk. That's why I wanted to write all this down, in case anyone needs to know what happened.

So that's it I guess, I'd better be off. The sun's going down, it'll be full dark by the time I get out to Bo's Grandma's place, and I don't want to keep Darin waiting.

Try to Remember

I need to tell you something, before it's too late.

It will start with a few lost moments. You walk into a room, but forget what for. Maybe you keep misplacing your car keys. Soon there are gaps in your day. Chunks of your commute are gone. Conversations with your best friend are forgotten. It only gets worse from there. You miss doctor's appointments, and your Mother's birthday. You think you're losing your mind, but the worst is yet to come. It all leads to… something. It's bad. I just don't remember for some reason. Why can't I remember?

Change of Season

The first morning rays were breaking the horizon and illuminating the scattered clouds as if the world was on fire. Lynn shielded her eyes and checked the clock on the dash for the third time in five minutes. Jordan was almost half an hour late. Lynn leaned back in her seat, wishing she had hit the snooze button a few more times. Nobody deserves to be out of the house at five o'clock on a chilly autumn morning only to be stood up.

There wasn't much for scenery at the timeworn roadside truck stop. It was on a flat stretch just outside of the city. Most likely built in the fifties, the plain cinderblock building with flaking white paint held a family restaurant and a small convenience store tucked off to one side. Four tired fuel pumps sat out front of the shared entrance. In a world of marketing and brand recognition it was truly just a place to stop because you needed fuel or a quick bite to eat.

Lynn turned the radio down and leaned her forearms against the steering wheel. She wondered if she'd be home in time to meet Cary, if she should call him to cancel. She watched the other highway travelers and speculated about their lives as they came and went.

Sitting at a window seat in the restaurant was an older gentleman hunched over his breakfast special. His leathery face was hidden by an unkempt grey beard, his tired eyes keeping watch over the Peterbilt parked out by the exit. What if he was a poet, creating works that would rival the masters, but too insecure to share with the world? On his way back to an immaculate BMW was a well-dressed business type, a to-go cup in one hand and a smile on his face. What if he had just told his boss to shove it and left his nagging socialite wife the keys to their downtown apartment so he could run off and start over with his high school sweetheart? It made Lynn stop for a moment and ponder what someone would think of her, a young woman sitting impatiently behind the wheel of her little Mazda, a stone's throw from the middle of nowhere.

Lynn had recently accepted a job at Hemmett Supply Co. as support for the out of town sales group. It was grunt work, but for the most part she enjoyed it. With one exception, everything was going well. Lynn's first solo project was a proposal for a new customer. One of the vendors submitted incorrect information, and it led to Hemmett losing the bid. Lynn's boss, John, was upset but understanding. Jordan, who had championed the account, was furious. He had screamed at her on the phone for almost ten minutes straight.

Lynn did her best to give Jordan a wide berth for weeks after the incident. She did what she always had in that type of situation, she put her head down and got to work. Lynn focused on building relationships with the rest of the team and helping them grow their business. It wasn't long before she got the call,

Jordan wanted her to come out for a ride-along. John thought it was a good way to mend some fences. How could she say no?

Any hope of escaping the day's adventure vanished as Jordan's Acura barreled into the parking lot at a reckless velocity. Lynn exited her car and locked the doors as he pulled up beside. Jordan called from his open window. "Hey, buddy!"

"Hi, Jordan."

"You ready to go? Big day ahead of us, I'm really excited to have you out here!"

"Happy to be here," Lynn said with a forced smile.

Lynn opened the passenger door of the RDX, dropped her laptop bag in the foot well and her water bottle into the door pocket. The cold leather seat creaked as she sat down and buckled up. Even with the window down, the aroma of last night's intoxication still lingered. The oversized sunglasses Jordan wore concealed them but Lynn could imagine heavy lids with blood shot eyes beneath. Jordan shifted the car into drive and then accelerated out of the parking lot and onto the highway.

"Thanks again for coming out, been waiting a long time for this. Here, I brought you a coffee."

Jordan grabbed a travel mug from the center console and forced it into Lynn's hand. Not wanting to be rude she took a swig. The coffee was bitter and had a strange aftertaste.

"Do you like it? It's my special blend," Jordan said.

Lynn looked sidelong at Jordan. "It's nice, thank you."

Jordan had one arm draped over the steering wheel as he explained who they would be seeing and what issues might be brought up. They discussed office politics, but it was mostly Jordan complaining about how terrible everyone was. Soon enough they ran out of things to say, so sat in silence as the landscape rolled past.

The sun was creeping higher in the sky, flashing in and out of view between the trees that lined the road. Slender pine trees pointed tall toward the heavens, aspens with their changing leaves signaled the new season. Lynn was watching the tree line, hoping to see some of the local wildlife, when Jordan broke the silence.

"So what made you come out here anyway? You're from the coast right?"

"Most recently, but that's not really where I'm from. I like to move around, experience new things."

"You're not running from anything, are you?"

"No. Just trying to find myself, I guess."

Lynn reached out for the armrest of the passenger side door. She felt light-headed, it was hard to focus. She shook her head gently and blinked a few times, trying to drive the sensation away.

"Just in time," Jordan said with a satisfied grin.

Lynn's vision blurred to the point she could only see patches of light and shadow. She tried to move or speak but her body refused to respond. The car slowed and made a sharp right hand turn. She heard and felt as the tires of the car moved onto a gravel road, and then everything went black.

*

Lynn forced her eyes open. It took a moment for them to adjust. She was laying on a tarp which covered an unforgiving wood floor. The room was cold and dimly lit. Her coat and boots had been removed, her hands tied behind her back, and legs bound at the ankles. The rope was coarse and tightly wrapped, the pressure was uncomfortable. In front of her was a worn leather recliner and a simple looking end table with an old lamp on top that had a large bear figure at the base. The window above the recliner was obscured by plastic and faded curtains which gave only an impression of the trees beyond.

Lynn began to shiver, her breath ragged. Trying to get herself under control she became aware of someone rustling around just out of sight. It was then that Jordan ambled in front of her with a brief look back. Lynn's first instinct was to shut her eyes, to buy some time, but instead she held Jordan's gaze.

"Oh good, you're awake. Can I get you anything? Another coffee maybe?" Jordan laughed low and continued on his way. "That was rhetorical by the way."

Lynn's voice was strained. "You're making a mistake."

79

"Shut your mouth. I know what I'm doing."

Jordan came back to Lynn, fumbled to attach a sheathed hunting knife to his belt, and knelt down inches from her face.

"Let me explain something to you. Things are hard out here. My customers are struggling to stay in business which means more pressure on me. I bust my ass twelve to fourteen hours a day just to keep up. And then to top it all off, I get people like you coming in and making it worse!"

Lynn turned from his harsh gaze. "I'm sorry, I didn't mean to..."

"Shut up!" Jordan roared and then stood. "You're useless! A waste of space! It'll be the last time you cause trouble for me though."

As Jordan moved back across the room Lynn swiveled her head to follow his path, he stopped in front of a large metal cabinet and threw the doors open. Straining to see the contents, it became clear to Lynn how serious of a situation she was in. Assortments of rope, chemical containers, and tools were stacked inside. The tools were ugly, implements of torture no doubt built with purpose by Jordan himself.

Lynn started sobbing, she pleaded with Jordan, "Please untie me. I promise I won't fight. Please…"

Jordan paused for a moment, then turned to Lynn with an unpleasant smile and said, "Maybe. Yeah, maybe I will untie you. That could be even more fun."

Jordan unsheathed the knife and crouched down to cut the ropes from Lynn's wrists and ankles. Lynn flinched and a whimper escaped her lips.

"Oh, I'm sorry, did I get you a little there?" Jordan returned the knife to its sheath and moved back to the cabinet. He began whistling a chipper tune as he gathered items. The dull thud was soon followed by throbbing pain and his vision awash with stars.

Jordan fell to his knees. His right hand covered the crack in his skull, blood dripped between his fingers. With his left he fumbled for purchase on one of the cabinet shelves to stop from collapsing, but only succeeded in scattering most of the shelves contents across the floor.

Lynn dropped the heavy cast bear lamp, now bloodied with bits of scalp and hair sticking to it like grotesque fungus. She bent down and lifted the hunting knife from Jordan's belt.

Lynn stood back and scanned the room. To the right of the recliner and now empty end table was a small room with its door ajar. Inside there was an old army surplus cot against the back wall and a pile of clothes on the floor. Beside the room was a makeshift kitchen. The countertop was made from scraps of plywood. An old camp stove was on top, along with a few well-used cast iron pans and cooking utensils. Empty whisky bottles were piled up in the corner. A large water container mounted to the wall had a hose hanging down into an enamel basin. Just off of the kitchen sat a compact table and single wooden chair with Lynn's coat draped over the back. She started to move toward it but staggered forward as Jordan fell into her and wrapped his arms around her waist.

Lynn screamed. She swiveled, struggling to remain upright, and plunged the hunting knife into his upper back. Jordan cried out and dropped to his knees. Lynn followed up with a powerful kick to the groin. Jordan gave a sharp exhale and folded to the floor. Lynn waited for him to get back up, but he was still. She grabbed a length of discarded rope and tied Jordan's hands behind his back, and then looped it around his legs for good measure.

Lynn staggered to the kitchen chair and sat. She kept an eye on Jordan while she caught her breath. After a moment she leaned forward and pulled her coat onto her lap. Digging in the front right pocket she retrieved her cell phone. A single bar on the service indicator danced in and out of view, but she took a chance and dialed. After a short pause it began to ring.

"John speaking."

"Hi John, it's Lynn. Listen, I've been trying for almost two hours to get a hold of Jordan and I haven't been able to get through, cell reception is brutal out here so I'd like to make my way back if it's all right with you. Maybe I could work from home for the rest of the day?"

John sighed. "Lynn, I'm really sorry, I'll touch base with him and find out what the hell is going on. I know he's had a lot of pressure on him lately but that's no excuse to leave you stranded. I appreciate you making the effort, head home and we can talk in the morning."

"Thanks John, I appreciate it."

The phone fell silent. Lynn walked back beside Jordan and knelt down in much the same way he had only moments before.

"Well, Jordan, I'm sure this didn't turn out quite the way you expected. When you let the anger guide you, it makes you reckless. I'd suggest you get help, but I'm afraid it's a little late for that."

Lynn put the exposed tip of the hunting knife to Jordan's side, he recoiled and gave a low groan. "On the other hand, I am anything but reckless. I learned from the best and was a very keen student. They're never going to find your body, Jordan. Soon enough your feeble existence will be all but forgotten."

Lynn stood and surveyed the cabin, taking inventory of anything that would prove useful for the task ahead. "Well, let's get started. I have a date tonight and don't want to be late."

Michael

"Michael, is that you?"

"Yes, Charles, I'm here."

"Where… where are we?"

"In a safe place, Charles."

"I can't feel my legs. Why can't I feel my legs?"

"It's for the best."

"Is this… Oh God, no. It was you all along, wasn't it? But why?"

"The reasons why will serve you no purpose. Not now. Focus instead on what is to come."

"Michael, please, I can't…"

"I'm afraid you don't have a choice, Charles. You see, I've decided to make you my special project. The others, the cases that bolstered your career, they were gifts. I have decided you will not be like the others."

"But, Rachel and Casey, what will they…"

"What will they do without you? Well, let's talk about that, shall we? Young Casey, abandoned by his father, how long do you think it will be before he starts to act out, to get into trouble? And Rachel, she'll be so heartbroken, so scared. As young and beautiful as she is, it won't be long until another comes along to replace you."

"Don't do this, Michael, please…"

"Focus, Charles! You are responsible for everything that is about to happen. You brought this upon yourself, and on your family."

"No..."

"It's time. Let's begin."

End of the Line

I can't believe I'm lost. How does that even happen in this day
and age? I'm tired of stumbling around empty, unfamiliar streets.
I just want to go home. As far as I can tell I'm no closer to that
goal than I was when I started. I don't even know what time it is.
I check my phone again, unsure of how the battery would have
magically charged itself in the last few minutes.

Everything was fine until we got out of the concert.
James started messing with some strung-out freak who was
making an ass of himself by the exit. No sense of fear, that guy.
We're in a strange town, on our own, and he decides to piss
somebody off without backup or any sense of who this idiot is or
who his friends are. Well, we met his friends soon enough, didn't
we?

We got separated as we ran from the pack of crazies.
James went one way, Derrick and I went another. Somewhere
along the way Derrick must have ducked down an alley or
something. All I know is that by the time I felt safe enough to
slow down he was gone. Now I'm wandering around trying my
best to find a way out of here.

I've never seen anything like this place outside of the
evening news. Whole buildings boarded up. Garbage and
abandoned cars everywhere. Half the street lights are burnt out
or broken. Every shadow is filled with menace. Even the cops

seem to avoid this place. I try to keep my head down but I know I stick out like a sore thumb.

I turn a corner and see a group of people hanging out on a stoop up ahead. I stop dead in my tracks. They're eyeing me up like dinner is about to be served. I'm stepping back when the winding down of a tired diesel engine catches my attention.

Pulling up to a red light just behind me is an old city bus. A thick layer of dust and road grime covers dents and peeling paint, but the 'In Service' sign is still lit up in the windshield, so I take a chance and run for it. I bang on the doors, praying the driver will let me in. They part with a metallic whine and I scramble up the steps.

I dig through my pockets and drop a random handful of coins into the collection machine. The driver doesn't look away from the road as I make my way past. I grab a seat near the front as the red glare through the windshield turns to green and the bus accelerates into the intersection.

The relief I felt at finding a way out of my predicament fades as I look around the passenger compartment. Fluorescent lights flicker as the bus rocks through the potholes and uneven pavement of the winding inner city streets. The maps pasted to the walls are unreadable from fading and graffiti. The seats are stained and uncomfortable. It's cold and dirty. There's an odd smell that I can't place, but it turns my stomach. There are only a few other passengers aboard, none willing to get too close to each other.

An old man is sitting on the sideways-facing bench behind the driver. He's wearing multiple layers of clothing, all seem to be soiled and frayed. He keeps muttering under his breath and shaking his head back and forth while he stares at the floor. Every so often he looks toward the back of the bus, then crosses himself and shouts, "Spectacles, testicles, wallet, and watch!" Nobody else seems to notice.

Three seats behind me is a young couple. They have the feel of life lived on the streets. They keep their heads low, deep in each other's embrace. If any words are spoken it's in whispered tones. The boy looks back and forth to the other passengers as if he's watching for some unseen menace. Our eyes lock for a brief moment and I sense his fear.

Halfway down on the driver's side is a middle-aged man. Strands of greasy blonde hair hang down to his shoulders. It looks like it's been at least four days since he's seen a razor. His jean jacket is tattered and worn through at the elbows. A dirty brown work boot sticks out into the aisle, the steel toe cap shining beneath shredded leather. His head bobs in between bouts of quiet snoring.

Across from the rear door is a woman sitting sideways on her seat. At least I think it's a woman, the muscular splayed legs and hint of an Adam's apple make me second guess myself.

She's wearing a black pea coat over a very blue and very short sequined dress. A pair of high heels in a similar shade lie under the seat in front of her. Her face is buried in a cell phone, her thumbs dancing across the glow of the screen.

Sitting in the middle of the seat at the very back is an old woman staring straight up the aisle with a crazed look on her face. She's clutching an oversized purse on her lap. The bright floral print on her dress seems out of place here. Her curly silver hair is cropped short and surrounds a thin face with diminutive features. Her beige orthopedic shoes dangle just above the worn rubber mat of the floor. When she notices me looking her way, the smile widens and she nods in my direction.

The bus travels four or five blocks before it stops again. It veers to the curb and comes to an abrupt halt alongside a convenience store with heavy metal grates covering the door and all of the windows. The old man, still muttering to himself, stands to leave. He makes his way to the door while watching down the aisle out of the corner of his eye. As the doors close he begins pointing and screaming in my direction. He pulls at his filthy hair and jumps up and down in frustration. The commotion is lost to the howl of the bus as it pulls away. I don't understand any of it but it makes me uneasy.

The bus reaches speed and the clatter of the engine eases. I look back to see the old woman sitting where the blue dress used to be. She's staring at me and smiling in a contented way. I don't want to show too much interest so I turn to face forward. I assume the dress got off at the last stop while I was distracted by the crazy guy.

I'm not feeling good. My head is fuzzy. It's hard to focus. I don't see any movement on the broken and cracked sidewalks outside. There are no street signs to show me were we might be or where we are going. The bus driver, faceless in the reflection of the front windscreen, simply goes through the motions as I assume he has a thousand nights before.

I hear someone whistling behind me. The old woman has moved up toward the middle of the bus. She seems different somehow, but the smile is still the same. Her purse sits open beside her by the edge of the seat. Her orthopedic shoes are planted firmly on the floor and her knees are close together as she focuses her attention on her lap. She's mending a jean jacket with a large hooked needle, but it's not a needle really. It is a warm white colour and has a rawness to it. The spun thread glistens as her hand moves up and down in rhythmic, fluid motions. It's the same dirty blonde as the man whose seat she has taken. She's patching the elbows of a jacket with scraps of light-coloured material. Something like leather, but not.

I'm fighting to remain conscious as the bus rolls on. I fumble for my phone, but it drops to the floor. I make no attempt to retrieve it, I'm afraid I'll pass out if I bend down. The out of service sign flips over in the reflection on the front windshield. I make a move to stand, to confront the driver or to find a way out, but my limbs are numb as the unusual smell overpowers me.

I turn to see the old woman three seats behind me. She's licking something glossy and red from her fingers, savouring it. Her face is bloated and covered in perspiration. Her skin is a sickening yellow colour. The curls in her hair are wild and seem to move as if alive. Her floral print dress is dark and stained; it is stretched to its limits by the bulging form underneath. I gaze into her eyes. They are black and glossy in the dim light. They seem endless. She smiles at me with pointed, white teeth. "Hello, luv," she says. "Don't you look delicious."

The Letter

Dear Phyllis,

Thank you for your letter and the lovely pictures. I can't believe how tall Cindy has grown! Such a beauty. I do see what you mean about little Tina, but I wouldn't worry too much, I am certain it's just a phase. The garden really is coming along nicely and your chrysanthemums are simply stunning, you must tell me your secret.

I am getting by as best I can with George being gone. It happened so suddenly after all, even I didn't see it coming. It amazes me how living with someone for so many years can change you. When I look in the mirror now, I barely recognize my own reflection. I know with good friends like you that I will find the strength to go on though.

The nice detective working the case stops in to see me every few days. He tells me he is confident they will have a lead soon. I'm not sure what will happen, but I do enjoy having someone to talk to. His name is Adam, and he's getting married to a nice young woman named Leslie next month. They're going to the Grand Canyon for their honeymoon. I told him to enjoy himself and to not worry about me. I said everything is going to work out in the end. And it will, as long as they don't find George's body.

I hope you are well, be sure to give my love to Felix and the girls.

Yours,

Deborah

Visions of Dragons

When was the last time you laid down on soft green grass and did nothing but watch the clouds go by? I certainly can't remember, but I did today. I'm not sure why. It just felt like the right thing to do.

When you're young you might see ponies or space ships. Harmless visions that spur the imagination. Today, I only saw dragons. Large and small. Fierce and content. Sometimes in battle or swift flight. Constantly shifting and contorting, they were formed by the clouds and by the spaces between them. They came to me, one after the other, for what felt like hours. I watched them and wondered what it said about me today. This worn and battered adult, whose innocence is lost, staring at the sky and daring to imagine.

I used to wonder what dragons were like. How they moved. What they smelled like. I often thought about where they went. I don't wonder about these things anymore.

The Queen

I sat alone in the waiting room. The scant natural light coming through the dirty window panes behind the receptionist's desk was casting grim shadows. I should have been grateful we were on the sixth floor, otherwise the windows likely would have been boarded up and there would be no light at all. A thick layer of dust covered every surface. Somehow it felt colder in the office than it did outside in the gentle falling snow. All of these things might have seemed strange not that long ago, but so much had changed over the previous few months.

The attacks started in October. Nobody saw it coming. How could they? Now life was like those post-apocalyptic movies that everyone used to be so fond of. Pretty much everyone I knew was missing or dead. Except for Jody. She's the reason why I was sitting in the dark, waiting for someone claiming to be the Queen of the vampires.

I was starting to get impatient when I heard footsteps coming toward me from the darkened hallway to my left. Jody emerged first, followed by the Queen.

Expectations are a funny thing. I'd had ample opportunity to think about what the Queen would look like. I heard stories that she had been in hiding for almost two hundred years. I couldn't even imagine how that related to her actual age. I pictured a frail, shriveled figure. The person who emerged from the shadows was anything but.

Irina's hair was long and black like a raven's wing. Her lips were held close together, and her emerald green eyes were focused on me without emotion. It seemed at first like a terrible stereotype that she was dressed all in black, but she wore no garish flowing cloak or tight leather. Instead she had on a simple blouse under an open button-up sweater, straight leg pants and reasonable footwear.

"Hello Marshal, thank you for coming," she said. I noticed a hint of an accent, but I couldn't place it. She sounded tired. "I am told that you have information which could prove to be useful to our cause." She looked to Jody. "I have also been assured that you can be trusted."

"I'll tell you everything I can. I don't really understand what it all means, but Jody says it's important."

She nodded. "You are lucky that Lazaro's people did not hear you speak openly about what you saw." This was followed by an uncomfortable pause. It felt a little like I was being scolded. She turned back the way they had come. "Follow me please. We have much to discuss."

Meredith

Thunder rolled in the distance. Rows of tightly packed homes sat somber in the growing shadows. The wind grew out of the west. The aspens that lined the street shifted and swayed. A pair of crows were agitated by the coming storm and circled overhead.

Meredith hugged her knees as she edged back into the embrace of the soft, brown leather armchair. Her oversized hoodie almost obscured her pale, round face and emotionless hazel eyes. She sat in the dark, the soft glow of a street light not quite reaching her through the living room window. The clock hanging in the kitchen behind her provided a steady rhythm and was the only other sign of life in the house.

The nervousness she had felt preparing for the evening subsided, whether through acceptance or the numbness of defeat. The task ahead didn't seem so difficult now. Meredith surveyed the aging townhouse which she had been renting for the past six months. Pale, bare walls surrounded sparse possessions, scattered about in an attempt to create a sense of home which had not been realized. She wondered what would happen to those things when she was gone.

Meredith grabbed a heavy crocheted blanket from the matching armchair to her left. It had been a gift from her maternal grandmother many years ago. In fact, she could not remember a time when the collection of now faded and worn pink and white squares had not been a part of her life. It was one of the only reminders of her childhood that she had left. She dropped her legs down, feet barely touching the floor, and draped the blanket over her lower body. She brushed the hood back off of her head and reached up to turn on a small reading light perched on the shelf to her right. Then she pulled out a note pad and pen that were stuck in the cushion of the chair, turned to a clean page and began to write.

I'm not sure how this is supposed to work. I didn't plan this, but I don't see any other way out. I'm not sure that explaining it will make it any better or if it will help anyone understand. Maybe this is only for my benefit. The fact is, they are coming for me tonight. I'm too scared to tell anybody, I'm so tired of nobody believing me. I just can't take it anymore. I haven't left the house in five days, I can't trust anyone. I don't remember why I came here.

Meredith placed the pad and pen on the arm of the chair and leaned forward for the mug of Darjeeling cooling on the coffee table in front of her. With the mug in hand, she sank back into the warm leather. She brushed a length of chestnut brown hair back behind her right ear and then cupped the large white mug in both hands. So many thoughts were running through her mind. Thoughts of the future, and of her past. She second guessed whether she had locked the front door, the distinct click of the dead bolt no longer sharp in her mind.

The blaring ring tone of her cell phone broke her trance. It was like an air raid siren going off in the otherwise quiet room. Meredith closed her eyes and let out a sharp breath in an attempt to calm her racing heart. The phone fell silent. She set the mug back on to the coffee table, pulled her feet up beside her and adjusted the blanket. Then she leaned over the note pad, picked up the pen, and continued writing.

It started almost two weeks ago. Weird noises. Seeing things out of the corner of my eye. I thought I was imagining it at first. Eventually though, I began to hear them in the back of my mind, taunting me. A few days ago I saw them for the first time. They're horrible. I'm so scared. I don't know what to do.

Wind battered the living room window and the first drops of rain began to fall. Meredith looked up and stifled a scream. Through the sheer curtains she could see eyes peering in from the night. The large moss green orbs were mottled with flecks of black and had jagged split pupils. They twitched back and forth as they scanned the room. Meredith sat trembling, her breath coming in short bursts. She peered over the half wall behind her to the window above the kitchen sink, and to the small window high in the back door. They too were filled with searching eyes. We know you're here, she heard them say. We're coming for you.

Meredith jammed the note pad and pen between her thigh and the arm of the chair. She pulled two cobalt blue pill bottles from the front pocket of her hoodie onto the blanket. Tears were streaming down her face as she removed the lid from the smaller bottle. She grabbed the mug of tea, put the open pill bottle to her lips and emptied the contents into her mouth. She drew deeply from the mug, fighting the tremors in her hands, and washed down the powdery mess. She winced as the sickening metallic taste overtook her. She repeated with the second bottle, but her aim faltered. Some of the pills missed their mark and fell onto her lap to be obscured in the gaps of the blanket. She chewed the mouthful of capsules and followed again with the tea, draining the mug. Meredith fumbled for the note pad and pen one last time.

They're outside, telling me what they're going to do. They know I'm special. They want my power. But I won't let them have it. They know what I've done but it's already to late there angry   I wont let them get me   Im sorry

Meredith dropped the pen and paper to the floor and then curled in on herself. She pulled the hood over her head and the blanket up to her quivering chin. The dull throbbing of the creatures rage began to drift away. Her eyelids became heavy. On the edge of consciousness, she heard a loud booming which at first she took to be the rumble of thunder, but soon realized it was coming from the front door. After a moment the cacophony relented. In a brief moment of silence she heard the click of the deadbolt, and then nothing.

Long Day at the Office

I wake up in front of the TV. The glare of the screen is harsh as my eyes adjust. A beautiful woman is telling me she wants to chat. All I have to do is call the number on the screen.

The wounds on my hands are itchy. Tonight took a lot out of me. I'm not as young as I used to be. If I wasn't so tired, I probably wouldn't have been so sloppy. I try to think about where things went wrong, but my eyelids are heavy. Before I know it, the darkness takes me again.

The Flood

Prologue

John sat on the front porch, hunched forward with his elbows on his knees. A figure shuffled down the laneway, silhouetted by the deep hues of the setting sun. William raised a hand in greeting as he neared.

"Evenin', Will."

"Evenin', John. So, it's ready is it?"

"Suppose so. Come have a look."

John led William around the corner of the house and through a break in the lilacs. A small round table stood in the center of a worn dirt patch. The same table that Emily and her friends would sit around and gossip over afternoon tea. That was a long time ago though.

John's creation was in the center of the table. It was about the size of a bread box, but not at all the right shape. Even in the long shadow cast by the house, the object stood out. It was vivid, like it was more real than everything around it.

John scratched at the stubble on his chin while William circled the table. It seemed like an eternity of heavy boots dragging through dry soil, but after a time William paused and bent down. He raised a calloused finger and squinted his grey eyes.

"Decided to keep that, did ya?"

"Made sense at the time."

"It's good. I like it."

John pursed his lips and nodded. His shoulders dropped as he hooked his thumbs into the pockets of his jeans.

"So? Think it'll work?"

"It'll work just fine. Ya done good, John, yes sir."

*

There's not much but the sound of my boots on the gravel and the cicadas in the field. I see the orange glow from the radio just inside the barn door. It's never really turned up enough to hear, but it means John is out working.

I walk in to find him pushing a sanding block along one of the hull planks of his dad's old boat.

"You're back."

"I am, just wanted to let you know."

John nods but keeps his focus.

"How are things going out here?"

"Well enough, I guess."

I scan the walls of the barn, covered with tools and smaller projects in various stages of completion. Some dusty from neglect, some fresh and bright.

"How do you find the time for all this, John?"

"Didn't know time needed to be found."

"Fair enough. Still not sure why it's so hard to do sometimes."

John pauses, leans down with one eye closed, and runs his hand along the hull. "Maybe because we have to fight for everything good in our lives. Maybe, the answers are inside us, we just need to pay attention."

I drop my head and smile at my boots. "Yeah, I hear that a lot."

John lifts the sanding block and gets back to the task at hand. "Sorry to disappoint you."

"Not your fault." I look back to the house. "I should head in, make sure the girls are ready for bed."

"Give 'em a squeeze for me."

"Will do. Night, John."

*

The door slips from my fingers and slams behind me. I cringe at the noise, but the house remains quiet. The kitchen is dim with only the small light over the sink on. Colourful flashes and low music are coming from the living room. I pop my head in to see Zoe curled up on the couch, thumbs tapping away at the screen of her phone.

"Hi, Sweetie."

She doesn't look up. "Hi, Dad."

"Tess already in bed?"

"Yeah, she went up half an hour ago."

"Did she brush her teeth?"

"Yeah."

"Good, thank you."

I'm careful to avoid the worst of the loose boards as I climb the staircase. Tess is in bed, head turned away from the lamp on her nightstand. The journal is open across her chest, rising and falling with each shallow breath. I kneel beside her and reach out for the cover. Her eyes flash open and I freeze.

"Hi, Dad."

I pull my arm back. "Hi, baby. Did you have a good day at school?"

"Yeah. We made Father's Day gifts today. You have to wait until Father's Day to get it though." She smiles wide, tongue poking through the gap in her teeth.

"I guess I'll just have to wait then." I smile and kiss her cheek. "Love you."

"Love you too." Tess wraps her hands around the journal and closes her eyes. I pull the string on the lamp and ease my way out of the room, closing the door behind me.

*

105

It's Sunday morning. That means Tess was up at six, she got dressed in her favourite outfit, and made herself breakfast with whatever box of cereal she could reach. Now she's standing in front of my bed, holding the journal close to her, just like every Sunday.

"Morning, baby."

"Morning, Dad."

She's watching me, waiting for me to ask. "How is Grandma this morning?"

Tess smiles and clutches the journal tighter. "She's good. It's eight o'clock, time to get up."

"Okay, I'll be down soon."

"We need to make sure we leave in time, so we're back before Mom comes."

"I know, baby. Just need to wake up a little."

"Okay." Tess skips to the open doorway, but turns before going through. "Don't fall back asleep."

"I won't."

"Promise?"

"Cross my heart."

She gives me a tight-lipped nod and then disappears.

Sunday is the day we go to visit Grandma. Except Tess carries Grandma around with her every waking moment. She'll spend hours a day talking to the journal. At the cemetery, Tess will stand in front of Emily's headstone, not saying a word. I don't pretend to understand it.

I turn over and reach for my phone. It is in fact only seven fifty-five. More concerning is the text from Janine that was sent only a few hours ago. She says she's not coming. Something came up. She asks me to tell Zoe and Tessa that she'll make it up to them. Sure I will. Just like every Sunday.

*

There's enough coffee in the pot to top up John's mug and fill one for myself. I sit down on the top step of the front porch and hand over his mug. Tess is off picking wild flowers and tormenting the cats. Zoe just got back from hanging out with her friends, but she sneaks around to the side door. Still doesn't want to talk, I guess.

It's been a long day. John and I take a moment to listen to the birds and watch the clouds drift by.

"Looks like we're in for a nice night."

"Sure does."

"Listen, John, I know I don't say it a lot, but I really appreciate you letting us stay. For giving us a home. Especially after everything you've been through with Janine and Emily."

John is quiet. I'm scared to look at him, so I focus on a dragonfly weaving through the long grass at the end of the walk.

"Whatever happened, whichever path Janine chose, you and those girls are family. There's nothing more important than that."

John drains his mug and sets it down beside him. So that's that, then.

John drops a hand on my knee. It's an awkward gesture that means more than he knows. "Tell the girls I said good night. Happy Father's Day, Daniel."

John heads off toward the barn. I think about calling out, to return the sentiment at least. Instead I wipe at my face with my forearm, waiting for the tears to stop.

*

I turn into the breeze and let it wash over me. It feels good after sweating my ass off for the last nine hours straight. Don't get me wrong, I like to help, but John was pretty insistent that we get out early this morning and he's been setting a hectic pace since. Said something about needing to get the acreage cleaned up before the storm. My sunburned shoulders are a testament to the lack of cloud cover, let alone inclement weather. Can't argue though, John usually knows what he's doing.

I close my eyes, tilt my head back, and take everything in. The branches of the willow are rustling above me. A group of sparrows are chittering off beside the barn. The air is heavy with the scent of canola and dust. God it stinks. Summer is half over, and I have no idea where it went. I miss the spring. Fresh lilac blooms and cool, cleansing rain. The promise of starting over. Now everything is hot and stagnant. I'm over it.

Solid footsteps on the gravel break me from my meditation. I open my eyes to see John striding past with a long coil of rope over his shoulder.

"Come on, Daniel, only a little bit to go."

"Okay, be right there."

I turn to follow and see dark clouds building to the south. Ugly buggers. The wind picks up, it stings my eyes. I make a mental note to check the upstairs windows when I get in.

*

I wake up to torrential rain hammering the house. Almost sounds like it's going to come through the bloody wall. I reach over and check my phone. It's seven forty-four in the morning. Damn it, I slept in. Yesterday took a lot out of me I guess.

The room is dim so I turn on the bedside lamp and take a pair of sweatpants and a t-shirt from the floor. I check in on Tess but she's sound asleep. Zoe's light is off so I keep walking.

One of the chairs is pulled away from the kitchen table and an empty mug is sitting in front. The door to the basement is wide open with yellow light flooding out, so I make my way down. John is crouched in the far corner covering up a hole in the floor with a wood panel. His rain jacket is still shedding water.

"Morning, John. Everything okay?"

"So far. Just checking the sump."

I can smell the must and damp, but everything looks dry enough. "Think we'll be okay?"

John gives me a sideways glance. "Just got back from out across the way. Creek's higher than I've seen it before, and there's standing water in the fields. Have to see what happens, worst isn't here yet."

"Not good." I look up the narrow staircase. "You hungry? I was going to start some breakfast."

"Yeah, should eat, I guess. Be up shortly."

"Sounds good. Holler if you need a hand with anything."

"Will do."

*

I flip through the channels to get Tess back to her cartoons. I'm tired of the news anyway, it's been the same thing all day. Record-breaking rainfall, flooding everywhere, general mayhem ensues. It would have been nice if the girls had gotten outside for a little bit, but by the looks of it that won't happen for a few days. The yard's about ankle deep, and the sump's been running non-stop.

Zoe hasn't been far from an electrical outlet all day. Tess has been keeping herself busy. There's a cardboard stuffy hotel in the living room, and the fridge is full of crayon butterflies and stick figure family portraits. Surprisingly she hasn't said much about not being able to go see Grandma.

I hear the front door slam. John's back from moving the chickens to the barn. I stand to go see how he made out. "Okay, ladies, finish what you're doing and get upstairs, please."

Tess grumbles a little but starts cleaning up her pile of paper. Zoe snatches her cords and bolts past me.

John is sitting on the bench in the porch working his rubber boots off. Three sets of eyes peer out from the corner under the bench. Momma and her kittens. They don't come in the house often but know their boundaries so stay put.

"Pretty bad out there, huh."

"It is."

"Anything I can help with?"

"Not right now. Get some sleep, I'll keep an eye on everything."

"Alright, see you in the morning."

*

111

At first I think I'm in that space between waking and dreams. There are soft creaking noises and a sensation of pressure that's unusual. It's the smell that gets to me. I open my eyes to a strange reflection on the ceiling and everything comes together.

Adrenalin hits and I'm up like a shot. I push the curtains aside. My hands are shaking. The water is deep, it's almost to the loft of the barn. Everything looks calm enough, but that illusion is broken when a clutch of young poplars near the end of the drive uproot and drift out of sight.

I throw on the first pair of pants I can find and then run to the hall. Dark water is lapping at the first step before the corner going down. Jesus, it looks like it's getting higher. No time to think, I turn back, and slam through Tess's door.

"Wake up, baby, you need to wake up, we have to go!"

She mumbles something and starts to turn over but I'm already moving.

We have a rule now that Zoe is getting older, knock first. It's habit, so I do it now, even though I don't wait for a response. "Zoe! Get up, I need help!"

I turn toward the end of the hall. John's door is open. I have a bad feeling, but I have to check. His room is empty. I look back toward the stairwell. There's no time, I have to get the girls out.

*

I'm searching for an old duffle bag in the back of my closet. Zoe is at my door. "Dad, what's going on?"

"Get dressed, pack some spare clothes. Get Tess to do the same."

"Dad, but…"

"Now! Please! There's not much time."

I push past her and head back to the stairs. I take a deep breath and wade in. The water is up to my chest as I enter the kitchen. It's freezing, I'm having trouble breathing. I can only get to the upper cabinets so I grab what I can. It's not much, granola bars, crackers, and half a pack of fruit cups.

I stumble and nearly fall before I make it to the top of the stairs. My legs are numb. The girls are waiting for me. Zoe is pale, on the verge of breaking down. Tess is already there.

"Zoe, grab some blankets, there should be a case of water in the back of the closet too. Tess, I need you to grab the first aid kit from the bathroom, okay? Can you do that for me?"

"Daddy…"

"I know you're scared, baby, I really need you to do this for me though."

I dash back to my bedroom window. My heart drops when I see a shadow that turns out to be the roof of my truck under the surface. Just as I'm about to lose all hope, I see it.

John's boat is tarped up and floating just around the corner of the barn.

*

"Shit, shit, shit. Come on, man, you can do this."

I'm hanging out of my bedroom window like some stupid teenager sneaking out after curfew. The water is only a few feet below the ledge now. This is the shortest distance to the barn, all I need to do is drop my ass in the water. Easier said than done. Janine was the swimmer, I'm praying that I learned a thing or two from her. Alright, this needs to happen now before I talk myself out of it.

The world goes dark and cold. Can't breathe. Can barely think. I point myself toward the barn and start swimming. I'm pushing as hard as I can with every stroke, every kick. I think I'm making good progress until I pause to look up. Damn it. Not even half way there and I'm drifting off course. The current is stronger than I thought. Need to focus. Keep kicking. Bring the left arm over, then the right. Left. Right. Check for direction. Keep going, keep pushing.

I'm startled when my fingers clip the hull of the boat. I swing an arm up over the side but my grip falters. I try a second time and I find purchase. Pulling my fat ass up is a whole other situation. It feels like there's a thousand pounds of dead weight hanging on my legs. I don't think I have it in me. I'm shaking all over, but I can't give up now. I just can't.

*

Some part of me is holding on to the hope that the last few hours have been a bad dream. I've finally stopped shivering so I push the blankets off of my face and sit up. Other than the odd bit of debris, it's clear to the horizon. Everything is gone. The clouds above us are dense, twisting and curving with the air currents. I don't remember seeing them this way before.

After getting the girls I tethered the boat to the weather vane on the barn. That's what, twenty-five or thirty feet off the ground? I'm not even sure. We got out just in time though, only the peak of the house is above water now.

We haven't said a lot to each other since. Tess is at the back, curled up on an old tarp between a couple small wood crates. She's got her favourite blanket draped over her shoulders and the journal wrapped in her arms. Zoe is at the front, staring out over the water. She only moves to check her phone. There's no service, but it doesn't stop her trying. I'm bundled up in the middle, my clothes are all hanging along the side of the boat to dry.

Tess sits up and shuffles up beside me. She leans her head against my arm. "Dad? What are we going to do?"

"I don't know. We have to wait I guess."

"Is someone going to come for us?"

"I hope so, baby. I hope so."

*

The sun is just about to touch the horizon. The colours in the sky are amazing, deep reds and purples as far as the eye can see. It's beautiful, but I'm worried about what it all means.

Things have been quiet. Tess talks to the journal every now and then but does her best to hide it. Zoe is keeping to herself, nothing new there. I'm watching the horizon when I feel a hand on my arm.

Tess pulls her hand back. "Dad?"

"Yes, baby."

"I have to pee."

Zoe turns, her eyes go wide.

"Oh."

I look around the boat, for what I'm not sure, but sure enough I don't find it.

"Well, I think you're just going to have to sit on the edge of the boat."

Tess scrunches her nose. "What?"

"You know, just hang your bum over a little…"

She's waiting for me to finish my thought. I hear Zoe stifle a laugh.

"You know, then you do your thing."

She looks over at the water, and then back at me. She ponders the situation a moment. "You won't let me fall in, will you?"

"Of course not."

"Okay…"

Tess looks a little hesitant, but pulls down her underwear, lifts the back of her dress and sits up on the side of the boat. I put my hands out and she latches on to my fingers. She wiggles back a little, and then looks me dead in the eye. "Don't look!"

I turn my head. "Sorry."

*

Our first night in the boat wasn't as bad as I thought it would be. When I woke up I took inventory of our supplies. Stashed in the crates were a few tools, a couple lengths of rope, and some strange mechanical bits. I did find an old coffee tin which has helped the bathroom situation some.

For breakfast we had a granola bar each and a little bit of water. I'm doing my best to ration but the girls keep complaining about being hungry and I'm having a hard time saying no.

A pair of ducks have been hanging out about forty feet off the nose of the boat. It's a nice distraction, something normal in this whole mess. Tess is drumming her fingers on the side of the boat calling to them. "Come here, duckies, come on."

The ducks paddle around the same couple of square feet, scooping water with their beaks and quacking to themselves. I will admit that the idea of duck for dinner has crossed my mind, but knowing my luck I'd end up capsizing the boat and drown us all.

Zoe brushes a stray length of hair behind her ear. "Dad, can you pass me a water?"

"Me too, please," Tess says.

"Sure, but you'll have to share, okay?"

I reach back and take a bottle from the box behind me. I hear a commotion in the water. I turn to hand Zoe the bottle and see a lone duck take to the air.

*

It's our second night in the boat. I figure it's about three in the morning. It doesn't matter what I do, I can't get any sleep. There are weird noises all around us. The horizon to the south has a deep red glow. It's like perpetual sunset. I doubt I want an explanation for any of it.

It wasn't a stellar day. Tess spent most of it covered in a pile of blankets trying to get some rest or trying not to cry. Zoe stopped talking altogether after the battery on her phone died. I sat around and tried to figure out what the hell I'm going to do.

The water is still high, and it's got this weird smell to it. Every now and then a dead animal floats by. Some you might expect. It's things like water birds and fish that worry me.

Whatever is going on out there, we seem to be the only ones who made it. Zoe thought she heard a helicopter earlier but it's hard to know if it was real or wishful thinking. Even if help is coming, how long will it take for them to find us out here? I know we're going to have to figure this out on our own.

It's surprising how fast you run out of things to say in situations like this, how soon the words meant to comfort sound hollow. I'm trying not to lose hope, but I'm not seeing a lot left to hold onto.

*

Tess sits upright and takes a deep breath. She stretches her arms wide and then hunches forward. I almost think she's gone back to sleep but her head tilts and she clears her throat.

"Mornin', Dad."

"Morning, baby."

"How was your sleep?"

119

"Not so good. How about you?"

"Not sure. Okay, I guess."

"Yeah."

"Can I have some water?"

Zoe leans over and holds a bottle out. "Here, I've got one open already."

"Thanks." Tess drains the last half and then sets the empty bottle down beside her.

I focus in on the clear plastic. There's not many left. I'm struggling with the fact that something we take for granted most days is so necessary for our survival. A glint of something catches my attention just behind Tess.

"What have you got there?"

"Huh?" She looks down behind her, "Oh, that." Tess pulls a corner of tarp back, "Grandpa made it. I'm keeping it safe for him."

"Oh. Is it something important?"

Tess watches me from the corner of her eye. "Yes."

"I see. Well, keep up the good work then."

Tess starts playing with her shoe laces. "Dad, I'm hungry."

I turn and sort through the box of food. There's not a lot left. "Do you want a fruit cup? Last one."

"Okay."

Zoe shuffles forward with her elbows on her knees. "Dad, have you had anything today?"

"Yeah, of course."

"You need to eat something, too."

"I'm okay." I smile, but I know it falls short. "Don't worry."

*

We're covered in tarps in an attempt to stay dry. The rain started about an hour ago but it hasn't amounted to much. Zoe is curled up against the side of the boat. I can't see her eyes but judging by the rhythm of her breath she's sleeping. Tess is somewhere under the ball of blankets to my right. I can hear her whispering, whether it's to herself or to the journal, I don't know.

There's no wind and no noise except the steady patter of rain drops. I'm brought back to camping in an old canvas tent as a kid. I'm about to drift off when the boat shifts in the water. I've noticed it a few times before, things like tree branches or debris rubbing up against the hull. This one felt different.

It happens again, harder this time. Zoe is jolted awake. "What the hell?"

My hand is shaking as I touch my index finger against my lips. Zoe goes pale and shrinks back when she sees the look in my eyes. Tess is peeking out from under the fringe of her blankets but stays low.

There's nothing else for what seems like an eternity. Both Tess and Zoe are watching me. I realize I'm holding my breath. I don't want to look, but I have to know. I raise my head up and look around. Off the back of the boat is a distinct wake on the water and a dark shadow moving away from us.

*

We're out of food. Any trees that are still above water have all turned black. Even the bloody sky is wrong. Oh, and we're being stalked by some unseen creature that may or may not want us as a snack. Everything sucks. Every. Single. Thing. I don't know how much longer I can do this.

I'm trying to stay as low as possible and still keep an eye on the water. So far there's no sign of movement. This strikes me as being both good and bad. Sure, we're not being terrorized at the moment, but there's nothing else out there either. No ducks, no gulls. They're all gone.

I huddle back down in the boat and pull a blanket up to my chin. For the first time in my life I'm truly scared about not being able to keep the girls safe. Without that, what good am I?

Tess is holding the journal close. Her eyes are half closed, she's just staring at the floor of the boat. Zoe is running her fingers along a length of rope, back and forth. She's shaking. I can see tears forming in the corners of her eyes.

"Dad, what are we supposed to do?"

"I… I have no idea. I really don't."

"We have to do something. We have to at least try."

"I don't know! Stop it! Please!"

Zoe crosses her arms and turns away. Tess shifts over to sit with her sister, staring me down through wet eyes. Damn it…

*

The sun is setting. At least I'm pretty sure it is. It's hard to know for sure because it hasn't broken through at all the last couple of days. You have to pay attention to the subtle change in the colour of the clouds.

It's been hours since the girls have said a single word in my direction. Tess hasn't even looked at me. I got mad at her earlier because she was crying and I thought she was faking it. I didn't realize that her tears had run out. We're all dehydrated. I need to be more careful.

I've been thinking a lot about what we could have done differently. How we could have been better prepared for all of this. I wonder about John. I come up with scenarios where he's still safe, where most people are safe. Maybe even Janine. The problem is I'm not a very good storyteller. I am pretty good at lying to myself, though.

The wind picks up. It's warm and there's a hint of moisture that I'm not fond of. The clouds are shifting around us, twisting and turning in on themselves. Out of nowhere there's a flash of lighting that hits back behind the barn. The sky cracks like it's trying to split itself in two. I'm waiting for what comes next, but it doesn't come from the direction I expect. Something hits the front of the boat hard. I reach out to stop myself from falling but my hand slips.

*

I'm flat on my back. There's a trickle of warmth on my left temple, and a hint of copper on the air. The girls are screaming, but it sounds like they're at the far end of a tunnel.

"Dad! It's coming back!"

I feel more than hear the impact. It's like someone hit a tree with a sledgehammer. I manage to get up on all fours in time to see the creature's wake moving away from us.

"Oh my God, there's another one!"

I follow Zoe's shaking hand. This one is bigger. It's pushing hard against the current and coming right for us. I reach out for the girls. "Get in the middle. Stay down!"

The back of the boat lifts at least two feet out of the water and then slams down. I've got a shoe in my face and Tess is sprawled on top of my legs. Zoe rights herself and edges toward the front of the boat. Tess picks up the journal and cradles it in one arm while brushing at the cover with her free hand. I heard the hull give that time. I scramble to get upright and cold water soaks into the knees of my pants.

I think I've lost track of the creatures, until a bolt of lightning streaks across the sky and I spot them about fifty feet out. They're moving away from each other as they close in on the boat. Oh God, they're flanking us. I think this is it.

*

The first drops of rain hit my face. I wipe at them and my hand comes away the colour of red clay. It hardly registers. I've been running on pure adrenaline, but I can feel the tank is almost empty.

Whatever the hell those things are, I'm positive they're toying with us. They've been swimming circles around us and the barn. Sometimes they submerge to where I can't see them at all, but they always come back. They're trying to wear us down, and it's working.

Tess is calling to me. She's wrapped in a blanket, propped up against her sister. Her face is gaunt, her eyes are hollow. It hurts me so bad to see her this way that I nearly forget what's going on around us.

"Tess?"

"Dad, Grandma says it's time. It's time to make all the bad things go away."

She pulls back a corner of tarp. I don't know what it is, but the chaotic tangle of wires and repurposed machinery has John's name written all over it. It's beautiful. That's the only way I can put it. It doesn't make sense, but it feels important.

I turn at the sound of movement in the water. They're coming for us. I can see their eyes for the first time, and I sense no hesitation.

My hand is drawn to the red button set on one corner of the machine. There's an audible click as it hits home, and then the world is bathed in light.

*

I think I'm stuck in a dream. There's no sound but my slow heartbeat. I want to open my eyes but the light hurts. It takes a minute before I can focus. The sky is a mixture of patchy clouds and clear blue. There's a flock of what looks like gulls hovering high above me. I'm shaking from the cold. I can barely feel my fingers.

I raise my head and water drains from my ears. I'm facing out into the yard. The boat is still tied to the weathervane. It's hanging a couple feet above the ground, the hull rocking back and forth against the barn door as it's shifted by the breeze. The girls are sitting on an overturned cooler at the far corner. Tess has her arms around Zoe's neck. She looks at me and gives a sad smile. I feel something resembling hope.

I sit up with my elbows resting on my knees, and I change my mind. Everything is different. It's not just the eroded hills, or the garbage and the broken trees sticking out of the silt and standing water. The smell has gotten worse. To the east is a bank of smoke or fog, it looks like it's closing in on us. Out in the field I can see the creatures. They're pushing through the debris, looking for a place to hide in a world that is fighting back against them. I worry the fight isn't over yet, not by a long shot.

"What the hell happened?"

"No idea. Mark pulled me into his office and blabbered on for twenty minutes, and then he's just, like, you're fired."

"Son of a bitch."

"Right?" Kipp leaned back against the driver's door of his Chevy Cobalt. He pulled a pack of cigarettes from the inside pocket of his jacket. "I don't know what to say."

Pash crossed her arms and sneered. "You know, I bet it was Cynthia. She's had it out for you forever."

"Cynthia? Really? So twelve years is down the tubes because I wouldn't make out with her at the Christmas party last year?" Kipp dug a lighter out of his front pants pocket and lit the cigarette.

"Christmas party? Isn't she like eighty years old?"

"She's only sixty-three, Pash." Kipp half closed one eye and gazed off into the distance. "I can't explain it, but we connected on some really weird level."

Pash's lips were in a tight, thin line as she watched Kipp.

"Hey, she was hot when she was younger. You get a sense for these things after a while."

"Wait, did you say twelve years?"

Kipp took a long drag from the cigarette. "I don't even know why I'm upset. Shit, the things I've seen, the things I've done, and I couldn't do any better than a bloody fry cook?"

Pash looked Kipp up and down. "Seriously dude, how old are you?"

"I don't know that I'll ever understand this place. I didn't know there was such a thing as being petty before I came here."

"I was like, not even in kindergarten twelve years ago…"

"What's the saying? Something about a train wreck, or a car accident maybe. You can't look away. That's me, I guess, I didn't look away, so here I am."

"But you don't…"

"Even that shithole out on the edge of the Cygnus Arm. Bag of dicks, those guys, but at least they didn't pursue extinction on a daily basis."

"What the hell's a signus arm?"

"I mean honestly," Kipp exhaled a stream of smoke through pinched lips, "I've seen balls of slime that were more supportive of each other."

Pash's eyes were wide, focused on the pavement in front of Kipp.

"No really, slime balls. That was out past, what the hell was it called? I think it was in the Columba Supercluster anyway. Granted they had the collective acumen of paste, but they were good to each other." Kipp looked toward the sky and smirked. "Anyway, if I was waiting for a sign, I'm pretty sure this is it."

He reached into his back pocket and grabbed his wallet. He pulled cards out, one by one, and let them spin to the pavement. He palmed the last. Its colours were so bright it almost glowed, and it was covered in strange writing. He removed a small stack of bills and held them out. "Here, take it. You're a good kid, Pash, and I sure as hell won't be needing it anymore."

Pash stared at Kipp, her mouth slack. It took a moment, but she reached out and grabbed the money.

"Alright, stay cool, or whatever the hell it is you kids say these days." Kipp dropped his empty wallet to the pavement and then lifted the card in front of his face. He drew the tip of his index finger along a metallic strip on the edge. A faint pop echoed across the lot and then there was a distinct absence of Kipp.

Pash licked at her lips, looked to her left, and then to her right. She folded the bills, slipped them into her pocket, and then lifted the visor cap from her head and smoothed out her dark hair. "I think I need a day off."

Take My Hand

The sound of an organ pushes through the silence. Elvis starts singing. Precious Lord, take my hand. Lead me on, let me stand.

There's something in the background. It fills the empty notes. I try to explain it away as a bad download, but I listen closer, just to be sure.

The noise begins to push through. It's visceral, angry. It scratches at the back of my eyeballs. The more I focus on it the closer it comes. A voice, whispering terrible things. I'm scared but I can't turn it off. It's too late for that. Much too late.

Full Circle

An ear shattering crack rings out across the landscape. The air is heavy with ozone, but it fades as the fog clears. On the ground there is a circle of dead grass that is broken and flat to the ground. Inside the circle is a man, curled in on himself. His clothes are dirty and torn. He is bleeding from various cuts and scrapes that cover his body. He is shivering.

The man raises his head. His left eye is dark and swollen, almost unable to open. He shields his good eye against the light. To his right is an open field. Patches of snow still cover low spots on the ground. In front of him, and to his right, is a great forest. Young saplings, each with only a few bright green pointed leaves, line the entrance. The man looks up to the cloudless sky. He breathes in the fresh air. He drops his shoulders. Tears begin to stream down his cheeks. He made it. Somehow, he thinks to himself, this might actually work.

Holding his left arm close to his body, the man stands. With his right, he picks up the survival pack at his feet. He shoulders the pack, and then looks to the apparatus on his right forearm. The display is blank and unresponsive. Switches are broken and the housing is cracked. He wonders if it even matters.

The man steps away from the circle and toward the forest. He searches his memory, looking for a familiar cue. There is a stone sticking out of the ground just inside the tree line. He limps over and sits on a piece of fallen timber among the young trees. He sets the pack down on the damp ground. From an inner pocket he pulls a first aid kit and a small foil packet. The man opens the packet and crumbles the nondescript brown brick into his mouth. As he chews, he opens the first aid kit and starts sorting the contents. He ponders his next steps. Get patched up, and then get to work.

*

Time passes. The grass is green and tall. The breeze is marked by the sweet scent of flowers. Scars can still be seen on the man's arms and around his thick, dark beard. He is healthy, strong. There is still much work to be done, he thinks. It isn't the life he had once imagined for himself, but he considers it better than being cut short, and if anything it will give him time to find another path.

The spot has been cleared. Many of the saplings have been transplanted in what at first seem odd patterns toward the open field. There is a lean-to where the man sleeps hidden among the taller trees. A short distance away is a low fire surrounded with smooth stones. A rabbit, or something like it, sits above the flames on a spit. The man gives it a quarter turn as he passes by. On the edge of the clearing there is a stack of cut logs covered in broken branches, their leaves now brown and brittle. The man's tools are leaning against the branches. Along with the axe that he arrived with is a shovel and various chisels of his own design. The man turns to look toward the rising sun. He breathes deeply and smiles.

*

Seasons have come and gone. The man's eyes are still vibrant but wrinkles are showing on his tanned skin. Grey hairs have appeared at his temples and in his beard. He sits at the fire, warming his hands. Red and yellow leaves rustle in branches or shuffle along the ground as a cool wind begins to blow. Tall, dark clouds are building to the north. The man smells snow in the air. It's earlier than it should be, he thinks, but that's okay, everything comes in its own time. He looks over to his cabin, the finishing touches completed days before. For the first time the man has a proper place to escape the elements. Every now and again he longs for something more civilized, but he's not sure if it's because it's what he was once accustomed to or if there's really something missing. The man wonders, how do you quantify civilization in this place? As far as he knows, he is the only sentient being on this world.

He thinks back to the early days. It wasn't easy. Learning how to hunt, how to make tools. Always working on getting better and being more efficient. It was a struggle, but he made it.

*

Many years have passed. The old man watches large snowflakes fall from the sky. The snow is a blessing, he thinks. It surrounds the cabin and covers the ground, hiding a number of surprises that will help in the conflict to come. He runs a wrinkled and calloused hand through his thinning hair. His long, white beard shifts as he pursed his lips. The old man had often wondered what it would feel like, when the time came. It isn't what he expected. Not at all in fact. He is nervous. And old. That is the biggest shock. Regardless, he knows somehow that tonight the next chapter of his life will begin.

The old man pulls his fur lined cloak close around him and looks toward the trees. The forest is silent. It seems the birds and other wildlife know what is coming. The old man turns to walk toward the cabin. Taking a winding but intentional route, he arrives at the door and makes his way inside.

There is a stacked stone enclosure in the middle of the room. Orange light from the small fire flickers across stacks of arrows, bundles of spears, and piles of improvised projectiles. They have been waiting, for years in some cases, but the dust is about to be blown off so that they can fulfill their purpose.

Inside the front door is the survival pack, restocked and ready to go. The old man bends down to check the side pocket, as he's done three times already. The folded bundle of material is still there of course. A little something to help with next time. The old man smiles. He stands and lifts the ornate long bow and leather quiver from its hook on the wall. He takes a deep breath, pulls the door open, and walks outside.

The old man crouches low behind a snow covered tree. As he sets his gear on the ground there is a blinding flash. With it comes the noise, and the foul smell. The old man rushes forward, fueled by adrenalin, feeling more agile than he has in years. He looks down at the steaming circle in the snow. There is a man curled up on the ground. He looks up to the old man through matted, dark hair. Their eyes meet. It's a strange sensation, the old man thinks, looking at a face that he's only seen before in reflections.

The old man reaches out his hand. "Follow me. They will be here soon."

I take a bite from my apple and look around. There's nothing out of the ordinary for such a beautiful day. Suits and knee-length skirts, looking for some sort of existence away from their tiny cubicles and fluorescent lights. Tourists, getting in one last trip to the city before summer vacation is over.

A woman is sitting out on the grass. She has a bob haircut and a breezy, flowing dress. Her back is arched. She's leaning on one slender arm. I don't remember moms looking like that when I was a kid. The boy has wild hair and no shirt. He's collecting sticks and making patterns on the ground. The girl is lying on her stomach, feet in the air, fanning herself with a magazine. Between them are packages and containers filled with strawberries, grape tomatoes, and mini cucumbers. All claim to be organic. The cans of water have a name I don't recognize. The husband is sitting up with his elbows on his knees. He lost his shirt too. The bronze tint to his skin distracts from him going soft around the middle. I wonder how he got her to marry him. She has an air of importance that he is lacking. Is he independently wealthy? Or amazing in bed? How did they get here? Two children, only allowed to eat organic food, but increasing their chances of skin cancer by the minute. They probably drive a Mercedes and live in an air-conditioned house

137

with enough square footage for two families. I wonder about people's priorities being out of line with their reality.

Behind the family along the path is a metal bench. It's tucked away in the trees with plenty of shade. It's a busy day, but there's only one person using the space. I want to call him a kid, but he's probably early twenties. He's wearing an oversized black hoodie, dark jeans, and sneakers with the laces left loose. He looks at me, catches me staring. Through wavy blonde bangs I see his eyes narrow.

I turn at the sound of strained car tires and raised voices. When I look back the kid is standing but he's still focused on me. He puts his hands in his pockets and makes off in the direction of the shouting. Something's not right. I look at my phone. Damn it, I have to go.

*

I lean back into the corner of the couch. The remote is sitting at an angle on the arm. I pick it up and turn the TV on. News. Repeat. News. Bad reality show. Repeat. Okay, news it is.

There's been a shooting on the south end of town. Looks bad. Lots of flashing lights and police tape. The reporter says two dead, another in the hospital. Of course there's a bunch of people hanging around. Everyone loves tragedy, especially when it belongs to someone else.

The camera pans across and something catches my eye. I rewind. Pause. It's the kid, the one in the hoodie. He's off to the side by one of the ambulances. Through the blur and pixels I catch the look on his face. I get the impression he's waiting. For what, I'm not sure.

*

The rain is almost moving sideways. It stings my face and it's dripping in my eyes. Wish I hadn't forgotten my umbrella on the kitchen counter this morning. I hate the rain.

I check the lights again. The red hand becomes a little white man walking. I move into the intersection with the rest of the sheeple. I'm shuffling forward, trying not to step on anyone. A space opens up in front of me. Something clips my shoulder and I'm spun sideways. I pull my glasses down the bridge of my nose and look back. The crosswalk clears. The kid is glaring at me. He looks pissed. A car horn honks. He turns and runs on. I pull my coat tight against me and do the same in the opposite direction.

*

I sit down tight to the arm on the bench. I keep my hands on my lap.

"Hey."

The kid tenses. His eyes are shifting back and forth, I think he's trying to find an escape route.

"Listen, I don't want to interrupt or whatever. It's just, I keep seeing you around, so I wanted to introduce myself." I stick my hand out. "Noah."

The kid crosses his arms and shifts away. I pull my arm back, make like I'm going to get up and leave. "Sorry, if I'm bothering you I can go."

The kid looks at me out of the corner of his eye. "It's fine."

I'm not sure he means it, but I'll take it. I settle against the back of the bench. "So what's your deal then? I mean, you seem to be around a lot."

"And?"

"Listen, I'm not trying to pry. You can tell me to bugger off any time."

The kid lets a long breath out. He leans forward and grabs onto the edge of the seat. "I'm not used to people paying attention to me."

"Well, I can understand that, I guess."

We're quiet for a while. I'm trying to think of something else to say when the kid turns to look behind us through the trees. He's watching, or listening. He turns forward and sighs. "I need to go take care of something."

"Okay, no problem."

He stands up, pulls his hood over his head. "You can call me Mal." He turns and walks off toward the avenue.

I smile. "Alright then, nice to meet you, Mal."

*

I sit and hold out the to-go cup to my left. The kid looks at it like I'm offering up a dead rat, so I set it down between us. "I wasn't sure what you like, it's black." I pull out a pile of sugar packets from my pocket and drop them beside the cup. "Sorry, they didn't have any of the creamer cups."

The kid's nostrils are flared. He's watching people go back and forth.

"So, Mal. Is that short for something?"

"Yes."

Silence.

"Okay then. Do you work around here? I'm thinking you've got to be a courier or delivery guy the way you come and go so much."

He half turns to me. "How long have you…" He stops and looks forward. "When did you first notice me?"

"A few weeks back. It was the same day that lady got hit by the taxi."

He nods. "Her name was Greta. She was on her way back from the store. Picking up milk for her grandson."

"Oh, I didn't know that."

The kid pinches the bridge of his nose."Listen, why do you keep coming here? What are you looking for exactly?"

"I don't know. I'm just naturally curious, I suppose."

The kid nods again. He cups a hand over a fist and leans forward, his elbows on his knees. "You could say I'm working. In a roundabout way, courier isn't the worst description." He stops, chews on his bottom lip for a second. "Can I ask you a question?"

"Sure."

"What do you believe will happen when you die?"

"I don't know. What do you mean?"

"What comes next?"

"Oh," I shrug, "not sure. It isn't a topic I think about much, to be honest. I'm sure there's something after this, but what it looks like I can't say. Why do you ask?"

The kid leans back, stuffs his hands in his pockets. "When people die, there is a part of them left. You would call it a soul." He pauses, sort of frowns. "It's my job to help them find their way to what comes next."

I'm not sure what to say. I don't get a crazy vibe from him. He's serious. Somehow it answers a lot of the questions that have been rolling around inside my head.

142

He sneaks a glance at me, and then continues. "I don't get to all of them. Some refuse, or find a way to hide. They think they're hiding anyway, I always know where they are, but sometimes it's not a good idea to force people into things." The kid shrugs. "To be honest, I don't always have the energy to worry about it."

His eyebrows pinch together and he stares at the ground. I don't know what to say, so of course it's something stupid. "Sounds like a tough job."

The kid's face loses all expression, but his eyes tell me everything I need to know. "You could say that."

There's a noise like someone clapping their hands at the end of a narrow hall. It bounces between the buildings so I can't tell where it's coming from. The kid looks up and frowns. "I have to go, sorry." He picks up the coffee cup, pockets the sugar, and then stands.

"Hey, I'm around again tomorrow, if you wanted to talk or anything."

He purses his lips, nods, and then walks away.

*

"So I've been thinking," I take my usual spot, set the kid's coffee down beside him, "if you're the grim reaper and all that, why do you look like some homeless kid? No offence meant, of course."

I get the closest thing I've seen to a smile yet. "To a certain extent, you see what you want to see." The kid looks around, and then points to a woman in yoga pants and a low-cut sweatshirt hustling by. "When she sees me, it will be different than what you see. That guy on the corner? It will be different for him too. When you see us, you see what your beliefs allow, or what you're most comfortable with if there is no other direction. What you think comes next, it's unique more times than not. What actually comes next, that never changes."

"What is there then, after all of this?"

The kid frowns and shakes his head. "You'll have to wait and see for yourself."

"Alright then." I scratch at my chin. "Wait a sec, did you say us?"

One eye narrows. "There's two parts to that. I can be a lot of places at once, but not everywhere. At one time it might have been possible, but not now. There's just too much to do. It was necessary for the whole to become many. The parts have taken on lives of their own, but the purpose is always there, and the rules are always followed."

"What's the second part?"

"Mine is not the only role to play. There are others who serve their own purpose. Your people have come up with more than a few ways to explain it. Spirits, angels, or demons." The kid looks off across the park to a line of retail storefronts. He motions with his head. "Speaking of which…"

I turn to look. I don't need to ask about what. She's like a beacon in the dark. Tall, well dressed, moving with purpose. She comes up to a man waiting at a crosswalk. He's middle-aged, seems fit, hair just beginning to thin. He's staring out across the road. The woman pushes her oversized sunglasses up onto the top of her head and leans in. I see her talking, but my lip reading skills are non-existent. The man's eyes narrow. His expression is flat. The light changes and the crowd steps out into the street. The woman turns and walks the other way.

"Who is she?"

The kid scowls. "Someone like me."

"Does she help people too?"

"It's different."

"How?"

"It just is."

"What does that mean?"

"She doesn't play by the rules, tries to change things without regard for the consequences."

"And you don't? Change things that is."

"I facilitate. There is only one way with me."

"Why would changing things be a problem? Don't each of us do that every time we make a decision?"

"It's not the same."

145

I shrug. "If you say so."

The kid crosses his arms, sets his jaw, and then leans back.

There's a buzz in my pocket. I pull my phone out and read through the notifications. "Hey, I have to get back to work. I'll see you around, okay?"

He doesn't look at me, but he nods.

*

I can't sleep. There's nothing much on TV, so I've been watching a group of guys dressed all in black running around hunting ghosts for almost two hours. My head bobs and the news is on. I last through the weather update and a puff piece about a local park being rebuilt. I sit up to turn everything off and head to bed, but I change my mind as the next story comes on the screen.

A man died when he walked out in front of a commuter train earlier in the day. Multiple witnesses say it wasn't an accident. I can't stop staring at his picture. It's the same guy I saw the woman talking to. His name was Arden. I remember the look on his face before she walked away. I create a narrative in my head, and I run with it. I don't think I'm going to get much sleep tonight.

I zip my coat all the way up and put my hands in my pockets. The chill in the air makes me realize it won't be long until there'll be snow in the forecast. I can already picture piles of white on the park bench and lining the streets.

The kid isn't here today, hasn't been in a while. I'm about to head back in when I see the woman walking along a sidewalk across the way. I run through traffic to head her off. I put my arm out to block her. "Hey, wait."

She stops in her tracks, tilts her head at me. In my periphery I can see the odd looks from the people around us. Soon enough they start to ignore me like I'm sure they're ignoring her. They flow around us like water around a stone.

"Can I help you?"

"I know what you're doing. I've seen you."

Her mouth is slack for a moment, she's watching me. "I'm sorry, what is this exactly?"

"The kid, Mal, he told me about you."

"Who? Wait, the name, what was that again?"

"Mal, like Malcolm."

"This Mal, is he sort of like a walking storm cloud?"

"Not a bad way of putting it I suppose."

She smiles. "Right, got it." She looks down at the gold watch on her wrist, "Can we walk? I have somewhere to be."

147

I'm a little taken aback. It's not really how I expected this to play out. There's something about her smile though, it's disarming. "Yeah, sure."

I fall in beside her, doing my best to keep up.

"How much has he shared? Tell me everything."

I tell her.

"And you're okay with all of that?"

I shrug. "I guess so."

"Good. Well, first off, the thing about, uh, Mal, right? The thing about him is that he spends all day with people who are deceased. Even if it's a recent thing, they're still dead, right? That can make you a little… different."

She grabs my arm and we take a sharp right up a side street. "To be honest, I think he's a little jealous, but also just plain tired. Sure the work still gets done, but there's nothing extra. No support. No empathy. It helps to have a little compassion in those circumstances, believe me."

"Compassion? What do you know about compassion?"

She stops cold. "Pardon me?"

"I saw you talking to that guy the other day, he ended up killing himself. I can put two and two together."

She rolls her eyes at me. "Pay attention, please. The information you're basing your assumptions on, and trust me, they're assumptions, is coming from a flawed source." She looks up the street. "Come on. We need to get moving."

The crowd parts again as we surge forward. My legs are starting to hurt and I'm breathing heavy.

"I'm not here to push people to an early end, quite the opposite in fact. I'm trying to give them hope, to show them the way out of the darkness."

We skirt around a group of people huddled outside the door of a hipster breakfast joint. It's all skinny jeans and floppy hats. God, I feel old.

She checks her watch again. "Does it always work? Of course not. This world you've created is full of pressures, nearly all of them self-imposed. You cover the pain with a smile, or by taking care of others instead of yourselves. You keep it all inside and it festers. Not everyone can cope." Her pace slows, she looks me in the eye. "People are so shocked when it happens, say they didn't see the signs. You don't see them because you don't want to, or you expect someone else to step in. Well, that's me, but I can only do so much."

We come to a stop beside a construction zone sign and a cluster of bright orange pylons. There's plenty of noise and commotion surrounding us. Heavy equipment and big trucks. We're on the bad end of the downtown core. Maybe bad isn't the right way to put it, at least not anymore. The abandoned warehouses and red brick office buildings are being transformed into craft breweries and handmade soap shops. Some call it progress.

There's a small bridge on the opposite corner. Traffic is light. I assume people want to avoid the construction. The paint on the metal railing is peeling. The concrete is cracked and stained. There's a girl standing on the far side. She's facing out over the railing. Her dark hair is shifting in the breeze, obscuring her face. She's holding her shoes in one hand.

The woman puts her hand on my back. "Listen, I hope we can talk again. It's not every day these opportunities come along, right?" She turns toward the bridge. "I just wish I wasn't so busy." When she looks back at me, her eyes are soft. "Take care of yourself, okay?"

The woman crosses the street and walks up beside the girl. They stand for a moment, looking out over the city, maybe at the decommissioned railway tracks below.

I think back to all of the strained smiles or tear filled eyes. I remember being embarrassed, or thinking that it wouldn't do any good to say something. Things always work themselves out, right? I know better than that now.

On the bridge, the woman tucks a lock of hair behind her ear and turns to look at the girl. A sad smile comes to her face and she whispers something in the girl's ear.

Acknowledgements

When I started this project I didn't know a lot of things. The insane amount of stress and anxiety I would have to deal with, the overwhelming amount of support I would get to help me bring it all together, or that the most rewarding part of the journey would be seeing my friends open or expand their creative hearts. I am lucky to have a lot of amazing people in my life, and I would like to take this opportunity to show my appreciation to a few of them.

To Ann, Tandy, and the other members of the Airdrie Writers Group, I would never have had the courage or knowledge to make this book a reality without your support and inspiration. Thank you.

To Renee, thank you for making my first experience with an editor a positive one, and for giving me the direction I needed to make these stories all that they could be.

To Sarah Ng, thank you for making the design of the cover one of a kind, and for showing me how the world sees me. You are amazing.

To Sarah Burk, thank you for your computer wizardry, for bringing my vision of the cover into the world, and for making it so much more than I could have imagined.

To Kaleigh, thank you for your encouragement, for keeping me on track, and for the most part sane. As far as creative endeavours go I know that this is only the beginning, for you and for me. I can't wait for the world to see how bright you can shine.

To Alicia, thank you for giving me the support I need to spread my wings, and the space to follow what some may look at as a crazy dream. I've never been able to find the words to show you how much your support has meant to me over the years. I'm beginning to think it's because they don't exist, that it's not possible to explain something that is so important. Or maybe I'm not good enough. Not yet. I love you.

To you, whoever you are, wherever you are, thank you for reading my stories. I hope you found something that made your day better. I am very proud of this book, but I need you to know that if I can do this, then anyone can. However you want to be creative, whatever your dream looks like, I promise you it is possible to make it a part of your life. I hope you find a way to take that first step on your own journey. There is still time. Please don't wait.

Coming soon from Shane Kroetsch

Surviving the Storm

The sky was overcast and the breeze light. Jacob had his jacket unzipped as he helped move food to the picnic tables. Clint had brought out an old propane barbeque and a couple extra chairs. Davie and Francois had cleared out the recent snowfall and arranged everything around the fire.

Jacob was removing covers from bowl and trays when the Millers joined the group. Darina was all smiles, waving to everyone as she walked in. George was a few steps behind, one arm looped through two aluminum folding chairs, and a large tray filled high with buns and sliced bread in his hands. Jacob smiled and nodded when he took the tray. George gave Jacob a quick glance before moving off to set up the chairs.

"I had just finished some baking before the power went out," Darina said. "Thought we might as well enjoy it before it goes bad."

"I'm sure it'll be delicious," Gwen said.

Clint bounced Hayden on his knee and watched Allena and Parker climb a snow bank while Erica dished up their dinner. Gwen passed out paper plates and disposable cutlery to the rest of the group while they waited their turn.

Jacob was impressed with the spread, especially considering the circumstances. Clint had rigged up an old oven rack at the fire so they could roast a pan of mixed vegetables and potatoes and to heat a pot of brown beans and a few foil wrapped empanadas that Malena had pulled from her freezer. Someone brought a green salad and a cheese plate. Davie was in charge of grilling hot dogs and kolbassa.

When everyone had their fill, Gwen, Malena, and Erica wrapped up what was to be kept. Nicolas made the rounds with a large black garbage bag for what was not. Soon the group settled in around the fire to talk and share stories, or in Francois's case the odd joke. Gwen brewed a fresh pot of coffee and a batch of hot chocolate for the kids.

The sun had disappeared and the firelight danced with the shadows against the piles of snow surrounding the circle. Harold drank the last of his coffee and set the mug down on the ground. He slapped his open palms down on the arms of his chair. "Well, I think that's about it for this old dog." He pushed himself up and adjusted his coat. "Have a good night everyone."

Penny stood and came to his side. "I'll see you home, make sure you're all set."

"For pity's sake, the boys brought more wood over this afternoon and there's food in the house if I need it. You've been fussing over me all day long and I keep telling you I'll be fine.

I've been taking care of myself for enough years that tonight shouldn't be a problem."

"Oh hush." Penny wrapped an arm around Harold's. "Let's get you home."

Harold frowned and gave Penny a sidelong glance, but followed as she led him up the path to his front door.

"We should probably head in too," Erica said. Parker was perched on one knee and Hayden on the other. She slid Parker down and took his hand and then lifted Hayden up on the other arm. "Allena honey, finish up your cocoa."

Allena was in front of Clint sitting cross legged on the ground carving paths in the snow packed grass with her mitted hand. "Aw, Mom…"

"Come on, I'm not messing around, it's time for bed."

Allena frowned and scrunched her nose. She stood and clapped her hands together to clear off the snow. Erica leaned down and kissed Clint. "Don't stay out too late."

"I won't."

"Night everyone."

"Good night dear, sleep well," Gwen said.

Clint waited for the click of his front door closing, and then reached down and pulled up what was left of the six pack from under his chair. He took out one can and set it between his legs. He peeled off the last can and tossed the plastic rings into the fire. "Hey Frenchie, you want one?"

Francois turned to Claire. She shrugged and looked away. "Why not?"

Clint lobbed the can into Francois's waiting hands. He turned to Jacob. "I can run in and grab more if you want one too."

"No, I'm good. Thanks anyway."

"Hey, what about me?" Davie said.

Clint cracked the tab on his can of beer and then leaned back and stretched out his legs. "If you want one you know where they're at."

"Gee, thanks." Davie stood and kicked at a chunk of snow on the ground. He walked over to the wood pile, took a split log in each hand, and then dropped them onto the fire. Sparks and ash flew in all directions.

Clint waved his hand in front of his face. "Come on man! What're you doing?"

"Sorry," Davie said. He sulked back to the empty picnic table and laid down on the long bench.

Jacob watched the embers of the fire and listened to the popping of the coals. A noise in the distance caught his attention but it was lost under the crunching of snow as Penny returned to the circle. She sat and draped a crocheted blanket over her legs. "Well, that was a nice night."

"It has been a nice night. That doesn't mean it's over though." Darina pulled her purse up on to her lap and took out a small bottle of Rum. She emptied her coffee cup onto the ground and then poured a generous serving from the bottle. "Don't be shy now." She passed the bottle to her left.

Gwen smiled. "Don't mind if I do."

Everyone settled in to watch the fire. Darina began humming to herself and then she started singing. It was a gentle tune, soft and flowing. Jacob didn't understand the words, but it felt like something a mother would sing to their child to calm them in hard times. He sank back into his chair, and half closed his eyes.

The sound of footsteps on snow broke Jacob from his trance. It took a moment before he saw a figure coming down the road. He set his coffee mug on the arm of his chair and leaned forward. One figure turned into two, and then three. Jacob stood, watching the group make their way down the ruts in the snow. The others took notice then. Darina's tune trailed off into silence.

Gwen called out. "Good lord, what are you all doing walking around in the middle of the night?"

Jacob counted five in all as they neared. They moved in a loose pack with their heads low and arms limp at their sides. Their faces shrouded in shadows and their exposed skin was steaming like a thoroughbred after a run in the cool morning air.

Francois stepped forward. "Hey guys, everything okay here?"

They didn't respond. The only sound was their labored breathing as they moved from the tire ruts to the path in front of Harold's house. They were entering the circle when Darina moved to intercept. "Come on now, don't be rude, who are you and what are you doing here?"

The first of the strangers moved into range of the light from the fire. The skin on the man's arms was torn and bleeding. The tips of his fingers were worn down nearly to the bone. Blood was seeping from the corners of his eyes, nose and from his slack mouth. It flowed down his chest, soaking into his denim jacket.

George took a step towards Darina and put a hand on her arm. "Dear, maybe we should…"

The stranger launched forward. Darina raised her arm to protect herself but she was hit hard and they both fell to the ground. The man let loose a choking growl. He clawed and gnashed his teeth as Darina tried to push him away. Clint ran up and planted his left foot and then swung the steel tip of his right boot into the stranger's temple. Jacob winced at the sound, it reminded him of eggshells breaking. The stranger went limp and rolled on to his back. George rushed to Darina's side as she sat up. "Oh my… Oh my God, are you okay?"